CW00857459

Pauline And
Her Petits Yiyis

I dedicate this first episode to

Bob and Sheila Rose

Chapter One

« Where are they? Where have they gone? » Pauline, a little French girl, exclaimed. It was not the first time she had experienced this strange feeling. She was alone in her bedroom, in the attic of an old Parisian building in the North of the city. When she climbed on her bed, she could see the skyline, the rooftops- with pigeons and stray cats- and the Eiffel tower on the other side of the river. Like every other evening, her father had left her to go and make a living, singing for tourists for the first part of the night, and then later for locals, into the early hours of the morning. She was not quite alone. There were many chamber maids on the same floor, Refugees from Africa, who had elected to come to France not so much to discover the luxury life, but more to escape war and starvation. They cleaned the houses and shops of wealthy people and that way, they could survive. They were kind to Pauline and looked in on her regularly when her father was away. Before, when her mother was still alive, they had a country house in the mountain. Her mother had suffered a car accident sixteen months before and her father had decided to move away from the past so, they had come back to Paris, where he was born.

Pauline was now wide awake. She had another look under the sheet. Mesmerised, she could only observe that her toes, her petits yiyis, as her father loved to nickname them, had disappeared! They had not been chopped off. There was no evidence of violence on the bed. No- just like bicycles which were no more on the parking space- they had left. She did not feel any pain. She closed her eyes and tried to think what might have happened to them. Had someone taken them away? Were they provided with a will of their own? Was she a kind of witch- she doubted it, she was a dreamer, admittedly. She read a lot and was doing her best at school to make her hardworking father proud, but to play with a wand and turn water into wine was beyond her capability. She had never tried it anyway! After a while, she finally fell asleep, only to be awakened by a soft muffled sound. As if in a dream, she saw the fanlight open slightly, and a procession of toes –her petits yiyis- the big toe of the left foot, followed in military order by the other four, then the big toe of the right foot, followed by the other four. The two big yiyis let the smaller ones *through*, holding the fanlight ajar. The last one managed to sneak between the pane and the sill, as the two bigger toes released it, and came gently down. The eight other petits yiyis waited for the march to resume, each pack of four led by the corporal as Pauline described them, faintly smiling.

She saw them move like little snakes along the wall, jump like springs onto the floor, move as if suspended in the air a few millimetres above the floor boards, and then, finally, climb onto the bed as if using suction pads, move beneath the sheet and return to their posts, like fishing boats returning to their allocated spots with the catch of the night.

Pauline was watching them, wondering whether she was going to wake up and whether it was real. Her feet were now fully normal. Pauline was staring at them. They looked exhausted. "How could they be exhausted?" she paused in her day-dreaming. Where did they go? What did they see? How could she communicate with them? They were asleep. Each reconnected to its usual position. She tried to wriggle them, their movement was a bit sluggish, only numbers two and three on her left foot appearing to react more strongly than the other eight. These two toes had always been slightly apart, not parallel, and the situation was almost the same for her right foot, which was a source of discomfort for Pauline when she tried to squeeze all of them into standard shoes.

Her father had always told her that she had lovely petits yiyis, like sea anemones, growing out of control, with their own personality. She closed her eyes and felt she could follow their trip of the night. She imagined the two corporals hitching the fanlight ajar, letting the eight would-be paratroopers through, onto the roof, then down the gutter and finally onto the cobbled road in Paris on that cool November night. She could picture them a few millimetres above the ground, in a file, following their leaders, two groups of five, hugging the pavement so as not to be run over by cars and motorbikes. At times she was blinded by the lamp posts, as if she was seeing from the top of one of them. How did they communicate with one another? Like ants? Using some kind of mind-reading? She could still hear sounds through them, as if she had projected herself inside them. The city looked even scarier from their small height. They were so vulnerable, but they moved quickly, with the corporals acting as mountain guides, scrutinising any potential danger on the ground and in the air.

They moved past the restaurant where her father sang every evening. She could hear his personal interpret-tation of old American songs, a sign that the Japanese tourists had not got back to their coach yet. So it must have been shortly after one o'clock.

5

They were now on the pavement, it comforted her that her father was there, working, not far from her. Then they resumed their pilgrimage. They accelerated, propelling themselves by a method unknown to Pauline. Were the petits yiyis of all girls, boys, and adults, provided with the same gift she wondered, or was she the only one?

After a few minutes, they stopped outside a tall marble building. There was a small entrance by the side, like a trap door, a few centimetres above the ground, large enough only to let them in. The vision stopped. How long had they been away? No more than 4 hours, she thought. It was still dark when she saw them return, but the traffic on the roads was growing louder, with the distinctive sound of the garbage collecting trucks starting their rounds at 5 o'clock in that area of the French capital city.

She had not had time to see any writing or markings on the building where they had stopped. Still, she felt comforted that they had not stayed outside, throughout the night on a weather-beaten cold street. She knew she ought to close her eyes again to get a little more sleep. As luck would have it, it was Sunday. Her father would have sung till 4 o'clock, and he would not wake her up at dawn as he usually did on school days.

She took a last glance at numbers two and three on her left foot. They seemed to wave to her. The big toe rose a little, as if to call them to order. Pauline closed her eyes, firmly decided to discover what was going on with her "petits yiyis".

***

Sunday was Pauline's favourite day of the week: she would have her father all to herself. If the weather was pleasant, he would take her to the Jardins du Luxembourg, where she could float a boat on the small lake around the fountain. Then they would attend a kind of Punch and Judy show, 'Guignol', a gentle boy puppet, always chased by a policeman, the children would join in, yelling to Guignol to watch his steps since the "gendarme" was looking for him with his wooden stick.

If the weather was not so nice, her father would take her to a museum. There were loads in Paris, of antiquities or dinosaurs, rockets, musical instruments, paintings and sculptures. Her mother was a tall German/Danish lady who towered over her father by a good 20 cm. When her mother was still with them, Pauline did not see much of her father. He was an interpreter and travelled all over the Western world and the Middle-East.

"What do you do exactly?" she had asked him once, when she had caught the word "interpreter' in a conversation between her parents. "When people don't speak the same language, I act as a go-between, I listen to what one says and I repeat it in a language that the person he/she is talking to understands. They are often in a factory, with machines and one person tries to sell one of the machines to another, who asks questions about the performance of the machine."

Pauline had always been a curious little girl. She tried at a very early age to converse with her parents with a bit of French, German, Danish and English.

"Why do you want me to learn English?" she had once asked. "This is not your mother tongue, nor Mutti's (mum's)?"

"No, but you will see that in most airports, in most cities, the signs are written in the local language, for instance Chinese, with English words underneath. It is convenient that if you don't speak the language of the local people, at least you can get by, order a meal, a room in a hotel, buy a train ticket and so on." Her mother had replied in Danish.

Pauline missed her mum tremendously. The summer before last, her mother's car had crashed into a truck in the mountains, in Savoie, near Switzerland, where they were then living. She remembered her father's pain over the loss of her mother. Overnight, he packed in his job as an interpreter and stayed at home. He would walk her to school and back, fix their meals and the rest of the day, he was pounding his computer, translating patents.

"What do you do now?" she asked.

"Same as before, except that I write instead of talking. A guy invents a way of taking better photographs in South Korea, for instance. He describes his method in English and I translate it into French or German, and I get paid for it."

"A little like when I do my homework then?"

"Exactly."

Today was a cold and rainy day. So he would take her to the Musée du Louvres, one of the biggest museums in the world and indeed, the most famous in Paris. They had lunch before the visit, this time in a Japanese restaurant on the long avenue leading from the Museum to the Opera house. Pauline loved eating out, trying out new ways of cooking, new tastes. Her father ordered a selection of sushi with rice and she did her best to use the chopsticks instead of the Western cutlery.

She watched her father enjoying his meal as if it were a holy moment. In the past, they would go to a restaurant, the three of them, always every Sunday.

Now, they were strolling among the sculptures and her father endeavoured to answer her questions. He never replied harshly, always bent on providing information that she could use in the class-room later. She was wondering whether her petits yiyis could benefit from the visit as well. Had she dreamed it all? She did not pluck up courage to tell her father about her visions of the night before. Would he laugh at her? Probably not, as she had seen him putting away robes of different colours into the wardrobe in her parents' bedroom a few times. The wardrobe that was now in the lounge where he slept, in the two-room flat he had bought on the last floor of the building where they lived.

She missed the countryside, the big house in the mountains and especially her Mutti.

Pauline was going to be tall, she knew that. At eight years old now, the top of her head was level with her father's shoulder. "Another 3-4 years and you will be taller than me" her father once said.

After the visit to the museum, they took a taxi back home and, like every Sunday, he would get a few books out. "Don't waste time watching television or playing with a tablet, an I-phone or a computer!" he would repeat gently, but regularly. "If you don't know what to do, open a book, about languages, history or mathematics!"

That particular day, Pauline could not wait to go to bed and try to stay awake as long as she could, to try and witness the moment when her "petits yiyis" would vanish for a few hours.

"Let's have a look at what you saw this afternoon," he said, opening a book with photos of the museum. It was like a quiz show. Her father closed his eyes, put his finger on a page and asked her to talk about the sculpture or the painting, not as an art expert, but simply what she thought and how she felt. Could she imagine what the painter or the sculptor had in mind, so many centuries ago- joy, pain or ....? When she was younger, it was her mother who would organise these quiz shows, but after her departure, her father had taken over. They often mentioned the past, but managed to stop, most of the time, before tears flowed down their cheeks.

He tried to make her laugh a lot, with silly faces, impersonating politicians and singers, telling jokes, putting a paper cup filled with water on his head and pretending to be an acrobat, with the glass eventually falling and he smiling.

They had a light meal and he tucked her in, time for him to go to work. One of the foreign cleaning ladies would look in on her on her way back from her afternoon-early evening shift, around ten pm. Her father would usually be home around 3-before the return of her petits yiyis, she hoped -and he would listen for her regular breathing before going to bed in the lounge.

Pauline sometimes heard the cleaning lady or her father and pretended to be sound asleep, so as not to worry them. Now, she did not want either of them to linger and catch sight of the petits yiyis on their way out or in.

Pauline's eyes did not obey her command and she fell asleep. When she opened them, it was time to get ready for school. She raised the sheet, yes, the ten little soldiers were there, in the right order and, apparently, sleeping like ten little logs.

Chapter Two

Pauline was a bit disappointed: she would have liked so much to watch the procession of her petit yiyis. She was thinking of laying some kind of trap, a harmless one of course, just a way of them signalling to her that the show was about to begin, without them noticing anything.

As he did every morning, her father woke her up and fixed her breakfast. Very often, one of the foreign lodgers on the top floor would take her to school with her own daughter. Pauline was two years ahead of the normal school schedule and helped the children of the newly arrived families with French. In fact, it worked both ways. She would travel to Africa, to the Far East, to South America, simply by walking a few steps, on the same floor. One door opening into its own little world, with various spices floating in the air, clothes of different colours, languages lIke Fula and Wolof with countless variations in over 20 African countries. She enjoyed picking up a few words here and there, good morning, please, thank you, good evening and her young friends corrected her pronunciation.

The school was only a couple of blocks away, a real melting-pot, with over twenty nationalities in her class, the last one before college. The French educational system was awkward she thought, with the numbers of the levels forming a countdown: after nursery school, came 11th class (or form), down to 7th. Then College, from 6th to 3rd inclusive, then lycée (after the Greek word lykeio) which included three levels: 2nd, 1st and finally, terminal (hence the name).

Her school was an old building, with high ceilings and high windows. This year, they still had the same teacher for all subjects, it was going to change next year, if she could pass to the next grade.

For the time being, she was with Madame Pelletier, the typical French schoolmistress, short with glasses and a limited sense of humour, no wonder, Pauline thought, with twenty pupils in the same room, only a couple of French origin and the others freshly arrived from various parts of the world. Many of these foreigners had arrived with basic knowledge of French, sometimes their parents were not very literate in their own tongue, but the young children would often work twice as hard and Pauline soon realised that the standard at the school was higher than in the countryside, in the mountains.

Should she share with Fatima, Nafissatou, Sarah or Zhi Ruo what she had experienced two nights ago?

No, she thought, it is too soon…

During the morning break, the girls, like all little girls in the world, would play with a skipping rope, sometimes two children held long ropes, then one girl would jump between them, soon joined by a second and if they could jump in rhythm, a third, and even a fourth would complete the team.

Most of the boys played football, others were engaged in a brawl about sweets or i-phones.

Among them was Aurelio, a little brown-haired boy from Portugal. He was shy and not too tall for his age. He had caught sight of Pauline's slight figure and long golden blonde hair. His mother lived on the same floor and a few times he nearly bumped into her, managing only to stammer a few words.

Aurelio was now circled by a few boys who were obviously not going to offer him a soft drink. He had a football trading card of a famous international striker that the bulky leader of the pack wanted. They shook him a bit, he resisted, then finally gave in, ashamed. He glanced around him, afraid that the girls, especially Pauline, would see that he was not the strongest fighter on the planet.

Pauline saw the scene. She had been tempted to call her four female friends to help Aurelio, but thought that it would make the situation even worse. Boys are proud and to be rescued by girls would make Aurelio feel even more ashamed. Apparently he was not wounded, perhaps a little shaken, just a normal, sad, day for him, but at least his honour was not blemished.

"I need to find a way of helping him, without him losing face," she thought.

***

The day went by, and after her father left for work and the mother of Nafissatou had made sure that she was safely in bed, Pauline tightened a little bell at the end of a short string around a nail she drove into the frame of the fanlight, that way, even if she fell asleep, the opening of the fanlight by her petits yiyis would cause the bell to ring. With happy anticipation, she went to bed, looked at her feet and switched the light off.

As expected, a few hours later she heard the bell ringing briefly. She grabbed hold of a torch that she had left on her bedside table, and was able to watch the procession of her petits yiyis under the fanlight, the corporal of the left foot leading the pack and holding the pane on one side, while the corporal of the right foot did the same at the other end. She closed her eyes and focused on them. She could "see" them going down the roof and gutter as before. They were now on the pavement and followed the same route as they did two nights before. All of a sudden, she saw them pause and hide behind a metal rising pipe, each on top of the other, barely touching the one below. A passer-by was walking his dog in the night and they did not want to be a treat for him. They waited for the dog and his owner to go away and resumed their stroll. They arrived at the same building, with the little trap door. This time, Pauline was straining to keep them in sight. They entered a large hall … She could hear noises, like rustling leaves, no, it was rather like thousands of grass-hoppers, or cicadas. It was dark and at that stage of her concentration, she could not distinguish what or who was there. There was a mesh along the side of the room, lit off and on by the headlights of cars driving past. She endeavoured to breathe more calmly, more slowly and little by little, helped by the rays of light projected by the cars, she could see a whole crowd of petit yiyis, of different sizes and colours, but all nicely shaped, and arranged in military rows, with a corporal at one end. How many were there? Hundreds? No, more than that. Thousands probably.

The cicada songs stopped; as in a concert hall when the lights go off and the musicians appear on stage, with the audience expecting the entertainment to begin.

She could hear a single cicada. Well that had answered one of the many questions she had. The petits yiyis communicated like cicadas in olive groves, vibrating at various frequencies and the sound waves were collected by the other petits yiyis who decoded them.

When the speech was done, all the assembly jumped up and down, as if spring-loaded, undoubtedly the way to express their satisfaction, like people clapping their hands or cheering.

Were they all girls' petits yiyis or were there boys' also? They were all clean and elegant. There was no nasty smell either, and most of all, there was no brawling, they were disciplined, as if they were all united, beyond any barriers of colours and origins. They were all abandoned and had to rely on each other to survive.

There was a sort of debate. A team of five took to the stage, and she could see slightly above the rest, in front of the crowd, a little shelf, with a team of five who apparently were running the show, like the head of a human parliament.

Several teams had spoken and now what? Would they vote, would they adopt a decision? Would they simply agree on the date of the next meeting? Surely not, she felt that it was an important meeting. Still, she could not picture herself talking about the things she had 'seen' with anyone, not yet anyhow.

Suddenly, the headlights of a car lasted longer and she managed to see that the petits yiyis in charge of the assembly were hers, as if the big one were the 'Mr Speaker', the next two were registrars and the final two were treasurers. "I am really going mad!" she thought. The vision stopped and she fell asleep.

She was awaken a few hours later, by the sound of the bell, and the noise of the garbage collecting truck slamming on its brakes. She opened her eyes and followed her brigades of petits yiyis coming back to the barracks. She inched her way down the bed, and sat on the edge, her feet now waiting patiently on the floor.

How would they react or would they react at all? How would they feel that for the first time they did not need to climb onto the bed and that the "mooring stations" had moved towards them.

She could see them in the faint morning light resuming their stations, in turn, starting from the smaller one to the corporal. Once they had all reconnected, she wriggled them. They seem to enjoy it mildly, but a little reluctantly, as if claiming some peace to rest after the events of the night.

"Hang on a minute!" she said firmly, "you owe me an explanation! You in particular," she added, pointing with her right finger to her left bigger yiyi.

He did not seem to budge. "So?" she insisted. And then, he began to vibrate, emitting a cicada sound, barely audible at first, then growing louder as she concentrated. Sadly, it was not like any language she knew. There was no way she could ask her father to buy a dictionary of the petits yiyis' cicada language and any bookseller would laugh her off if she tried on her own.

But, gradually, as she cut herself off from the rest of the world, oblivious now to the sound of rising traffic on the road below, she let her body echo with the vibrations produced by the left corporal. As if they understood the difficulty of the situation, the other four joined in and then the five on her right foot. All in tune, in unison. There was no grammar, no verbs, just images, turning into a video little by little. Yes, definitely, what she was seeing, through them, exceeded what she could have expected. The world was tormented by pain everywhere. She saw children fleeing from war zones, bombs dropped on villages, floods, forests dying, trees cut by the million, people starving.

And the petits yiyis? They had decided to try to make it right, all over the world, and rebellion was growing. They expressed the anger of children at the treason of adults. She could now see thousands of meetings of little toes all over the world, in secret places. "Right," she thought, "it's all very well to talk and dream, but what are you going to do about it? She saw herself, an older self, commanding an army of petits yiyis. Or, more precisely, acting as a bridge between the world of humans and that of the little soldiers of peace. Images were going faster and faster. Was it a projection into the future? She felt surrounded by a cloud of kindness and purity, instead of anger and violence.

Yes, she was beginning to understand: fighting violence with violence would only increase the damage. Only a gigantic wave of kindness and compassion could prevent the extermination of the human race and the death of the planet.

But this was a long way away. Right now, the disasters needed to be stopped, and this is what the discussion she had witnessed earlier was all about …

Chapter Three

« Papa! » Pauline paused a minute while her father put a pot of coffee on the table for breakfast. « What is God? »

He did not flinch, thinking that Pauline would inevitably ask more and more difficult questions as she grew up. There was no point in evading a reply. She would try again and again until she had something serious to reflect on, a little like a puppy who needs a bone of an acceptable size to chew on for a couple of hours.

"The truth is that nobody knows" he began, selecting his words carefully, not too many long Greek or Latin words that would not ring any bells with her. He needed to create a situation which she could relate to and chew on, to enable her to come to her own theory. "At your school there are many little girls of different colours who come from various parts of the world, right?" He had her undivided attention. "They have different ways, they don't go to churches like us, but to other places and some of them, perhaps most of them, don't have a place corresponding to their tradition, I mean, where they would go in Africa or the Far-East." Now, he could see her forming images in her head, Nafissatou, Fatima, Sarah and Zhi Ruo. She remembered seeing a hand-shaped jewel hanging around Fatima's neck, whereas Sarah wore a kind of star, for Nafissatou a cross, but Zhi Ruo was the most exotic, with a circle and the statue of a fattish guy with his legs folded under his body.

"Yes, they all have a different answer to your question," he resumed, "but they all have something in common." He was looking for a concept, a picture rather, that she could grasp immediately. "You remember Star Wars, the movies?" She nodded.

"When they say "may the Force be with you" it is a possible explanation. God is something we cannot describe nor understand. The Jews call him "ha shem", the name, other people say it is the universe and the laws of nature, why a planet revolves around a sun, why we can move on a planet without falling into infinite darkness. Some say that the world, the universe was created from nothing, others from numbers, others again that the world has no beginning and no end, others again have written about a great number of gods, with superpowers, living in another world above us, like the Hindu, Greek and the Latin civilisations and you will start to learn about them next year in College." She smiled, she could not wait.

"The main thing is that all of them teach you to try and be kind towards others. Not to be too selfish, to accept others as they are and not to judge too quickly. We all suffer, at various degrees and instead of adding to each other's pain, it seems more intelligent in the long run to spread laughter and kindness rather than wasting time in jealousy and anger."

He saw from the expression on her face that these words were sinking in slowly, and yes, she might let him off the hook for the time being. He had tried not to confuse her, just to plant into her brain that there was no ready-made, easy-to-digest answer to complicated questions, and that she needed to think, think, think and gradually choose what she believed.

"You mentioned super powers" He saw it coming and knew that he would be cornered, but better that than serving a white lie on a plate. "If God, or whatever people call him, created the universe and laid down the laws of kindness and help ...." Yes, he feared, she is going to tackle the topic for which I have no acceptable answer. "Why did he inflict so much pain to us? Why did he let mother die in the car accident?"

At moments like that, he wished that there would be a power cut or a gentle earthquake to take Pauline's mind off the present time, but no, the electricity board was not on strike, a rarity in France, the country of strikes, and there was no earthquake either, another rarity.

He rose to his feet, took a couple of steps towards her chair, knelt down and held her hands, trying not to cry. "The truth is, ma petite chérie, is that I - do – not - know." He said, mincing his words. "Being an adult does not grant you infinite knowledge, we, usually, tend to know more because we have studied longer, but an adult is not a super being, just a grown-up child who pays the bills and tries to educate the next generation with love."

"This is probably why the petits yiyis decide to rebel!" she thought. "Adults could help, at best, but they would not provide the solutions." She needed to cicada with her little soldiers tonight

***

Her father had left for work and now there she was, on her own, in the comfort of her bedroom. She had a couple of hours before one of the cleaning ladies would stick her nose in her bedroom, so she sat up on her bed, looking at her petits yiyis. She started to build images in her head, remembering them in the large hall, with thousands of them, communicating by vibrations. She wriggled them to attention. Would they need to disconnect from her to cicada?

That morning's conversation with her father had raised more questions than answers, but she needed to know what was going on in this under-pavement world where the yiyis met and discussed the problems of the world.

Firstly all of them were very unhappy, about the way the world was going. But what could they do? Wage war against armies? Convince adults to stop polluting? Were petit yiyis meeting all over the planet?

Pauline herself was a curious mix: her mother was half German and half Danish, and her father had Greek, Spanish, Italian, as well as French blood in his veins.

She remembered her last summer vacation on a little Greek island, Zakynthos, with her father's cousin. The people there complained that the winters were getting wetter and colder and the summers even hotter and longer. She heard the same complaints from her Uncles and Aunts in Denmark and Germany. The future was not looking so bright for the petits yiyis, who were the first to be affected by burning hot pavements or flooding roads.

Secondly: had they formed a central power, a kind of United Groups of Petits Yiyis, voting laws and having them applied everywhere? How did it start and who was the founder? A gang of petit yiyis in some part of the world who had enough of getting too wet, too cold, and then too hot for too long, who had contacted other groups and little by little formed a club, and then, as their children owners moved around the globe, convinced other petits yiyis to join in?

From the images Pauline had received, there was going to be a non-violent rebellion, without bombs and grenades.

She thought of the little Chinese girl in her class, Zhi Ruo, during the intermission at school, she would make funny moves with the other Chinese girls, slowly, all of them following an imaginary rhythm. "What are you doing?' Pauline had asked. "Chi-Qong," Zhi Ruo had replied and seeing that meant nothing to Pauline, she added "It was invented by monks centuries ago." Pauline knew something about monks: men living in old buildings in the mountains, away from civilisation, making jam and pottery to earn money. "To prevent them from dozing off during meditation…" Zhi Ruo saw that the word meditation needed some explanation and continued "You see my jewel hanging from my necklace?" Pauline indeed was staring at the plumpish fellow, sitting on his folded legs. "He is not sleeping, he has his eyes closed but he is thinking, focusing on one thing at a time.", insensitive Now, she was talking, this was just like Pauline trying to establish contact with her petits yiyis by cicada-ing , shutting out the hustle and bustle of the outside world. So Pauline had just discovered that she could meditate.

"I see in your eyes that you know what I mean. So'" Zhi Ruo resumed, "when young monks were called to meditation, some of them fell asleep, so a master had the idea of asking them to make movements with their arms- eighteen basic ones- so that they would focus on something to do and stay awake."

"But I saw you and your friend moving fast, several times, and a few times even fighting?" Pauline retorted.

"When we start to move and seem to be dancing, it becomes "Tai-Chi" and when we move really fast, it is called "Kung-Fu", which simply means "good practice" or "good work". It was invented by the same monks, to meditate, to focus better and to defend themselves against robbers when they went to the villages to sell their stuff." And then, as a joke, Zhi Ruo clenched her fist, directed it at the speed of light towards Pauline, but stopped a couple of inches away, without touching her. Pauline felt pushed behind, by the compressed air.

"Are you a magician?" she exclaimed.

"No, put simply, when you move fast, air can be compared to water. You know when you push a boat on a lake, by splashing the water behind it?" It was a lot to take in for Pauline.

She was staring at her petits yiyis. Thoughts and images were colliding in her head as she was trying to channel them in a vaguely orderly manner: Kung Fu, petits yiyis, cicada, focussing. She had not been hurt in the least by the air pushed towards her by Zhi Ruo, it was more like a barrier on a level-crossing by a railway track.

She smiled. What if millions of petits yiyis could learn to unite and push sufficient air to stop men when they were about to destroy nature or commit war crimes?

Chapter Four

« Papa? » Pauline's father did not know what was coming next. Gone was the time when she would come up with easy questions, such as "why are we still wet when the rain has stopped falling?" or "why do we have to give money for the food we have in the trolley in the supermarket?" At this rate, it won't be long before she asks about the difference between private and state pensions, the purpose of Brexit, or the reasons why Donald Trump had been elected, he thought, smiling - tongue-in-cheek.

"Do you know anything about Kung-Fu?" He was elated. Yes, it was an easy one, apparently.

"Yes, ma petite chérie." Pauline did not know much about her father's past, except that he was a few years older than her mum, 15 to be exact, and that he used to be a kind of solider before he became an interpreter and met her mum in Wiesbaden, in the South of Germany. Her father hesitated a bit, but sooner or later, she would have to know the truth about his past, so that morning was as good as any to start … a few drops at a time.

"When I was your age" he could see that she was really focussed, would she be able to imagine the fifty-one year old man as a little boy, with hair? "I was hyper-active, that is to say restless, I needed to walk and run all the time. I found it hard to sit on a chair for several hours and my parents had problems with the teachers. Not that I was lagging behind, I seemed to understand faster than the others I just could not wait to go down to the courtyard and run."

"So what happened?" she asked, her eyebrows almost joining above the tip of her nose.

"In those days, France was one of the first countries to have an embassy, you know what an ambassador is, a man who represents his country in another and acts as a go-between between his government and the government of the other country"

"Yes Papa, I know, I watch the news." Indeed, he was aware that she was pretty switched on, but better safe than sorry. "So," he paused to selected his words carefully "it was at the time when movies started to show mysterious fighters from the East, with new techniques, with the exception of Boxe Française- which to my knowledge was the only martial art, one century ago- where you can use your hands and legs to strike an opponent, a practice developed mainly in the police force." He glanced at her, and saw that she was following him closely.

"China offered France an exchange programme: Chinese children would come to France to study in schools and college, and French children would do the same, in China."

"So you studied Chinese when you were my age?"

Now came the tricky bit. "My parents sent me to a special place- a monastery, away from civilisation- for 4 years, from the age of 7 to 11. I studied Kung-Fu … and religion, well, sort of."

She thought of Zhi Ruo. The Chinese girl had told her about the meaning of the word monastery. She imagined her father making the same gestures as she saw her do in the courtyard, but as far as she could remember, she had never seen him. On the other hand, she had not seen a lot of him up to 15 months ago and even now, she only saw him for a few hours in the evening, plus the week-ends.

Pauline had many questions bouncing around in her head and did not know which one to throw in first. "Why had her father never mentioned this, was there anything secret about it, could he push air waves towards people's faces, could he command petits yiyis, could he cicada, and could she tell him about what was happening to her? She did not say a word and sat in silence, simply forming pictures in her mind, based on what she had seen on TV, on i-phones and her conversations with Zhi Ruo: young men in orange pants and shirts raising their legs high in the air hundreds of times while carrying heavy buckets of water, others jumping from the top of posts just wide enough to place a foot, and others striking the surface of tubs filled with water, for hours. Yes she could imagine her father, as a child, painfully imitating the Chinese boys.

"Yes I did all that" he said calmly and it was as if she had projected her own visions on the wall. She was surprised, but felt comforted. Yes, she was his daughter through and through.

***

Aurelio was in the courtyard, away from the usual bullying gang. Pauline walked gently towards him. He saw her approaching, checking that the gang was not in the area, in case they took a fancy to going after him, this time in the presence of the last witness he wanted: Pauline.

By some kind of coincidence, Zhi Ruo, Fatima, Sarah and Nafissatou were skipping rope in a corner of the yard, exactly in the area where the bullies were engrossed in a vivid discussion about the possible outcome of the game of football scheduled for that evening on television.

"Bom dia, como você está?" (good morning, how are you?) she ventured, all the words she knew in Portuguese, just to break the ice.

Aurelio was shaking like a leaf, but tried to stand tall and replied timidly. Pauline was a good four inches taller, at the same age.

"We are starting a Kung-Fu club with Zhi Ruo, would you like to join us?" she started, then added quickly, not to offend his pride. "In fact, we are all beginners, except Zhi Ruo'" She was not sure whether Aurelio would take the bait.

"My father says that it is a good way to learn how to defend oneself against several people at a time." He had never said it, but she knew that he could have and it was a white lie, a diplomatic way of teaching Aurelio to fend for himself, rather than to be protected by several girls, in front of the whole school. She was fully aware that he would not become world champion in two weeks, but she felt she could help him without being noticed, using the air waves, providing she could start to control them reasonably quickly. She knew some little creatures that could give a hand, but, no, she laughed inwardly, who could give a ... petit yiyi.

***

Zhi Ruo was all for it, to train the four girls and to include Aurelio in the club. They all lived on the same floor, in the same building and could train away from the rest of the school, especially away from the young bullies.

"You don't need to practice for hours in the beginning," the young Chinese girl said, happy to transmit to her friends what she had been learning since she was able to walk, "twenty minutes in the morning before to school and the same in the evening will get you going!"

Aurelio was intimidated at first, in the company of five girls, but as the first session unfolded on that cool evening, in the corridor where no one would pass before dinner, he started to unwind.

Zhi Ruo began with the eighteen hand movements: bending the knees, opening the chest, saluting the moon, separating the clouds, and asking her friends to breathe in by inflating their bellies, contrary to traditional fitness exercises.

Pauline felt more and more calm, glancing at Aurelio, who was doing his best to follow and gradually forgetting that he was the only boy. Yes the teacher was a girl, not a strong boy, but she was teaching her female friends and he was a guest, a complete beginner like the four girls, who also were doing their best to follow Zhi Ruo's voice.

They were asked to repeat each exercise five times. "You don't need to perform them in that order if you can't remember, just try to do a few of them on your own, a few minutes in your bedroom. A good idea is to focus on something, like the line of a poem or a maths problem, you look at it once and you start Chi Kong, with your eyes closed," she said.

That's a good way of killing two birds with one stone, Pauline thought, learning for school and having a physical exercise.

***

The evening of the same day, once her father had left, she was in her bedroom, trying to remember the various movements bending the knees, opening the chest, saluting the moon, separating the clouds, with one idea, one experiment on her mind.

She was picturing her petits yiyis, still attached to her, but vibrating, softly, without her losing her balance. She could feel the energy she drew from the air and that she was transmitting down to them, like an alternator charging the battery of a car. They would probably leave her in a few hours, for their nightly gathering. She did not know what to expect.

An awkward sensation rose from the ground throughout her body, or was it a dream? For a fleeting second, she was floating in the air, a few millimeters above the floor boards, with her petits yiyis vibrating like the wings of a butterfly.

She touched the ground after what seemed an eternity, but was probably only a few seconds.

She continued with what she remembered of the remaining fourteen hand movements, still breathing in while inflating her belly, then breathing out slowly, with the tip of her tongue touching her palate, just behind her front teeth. She missed out a couple, perhaps three out of the eighteen in total. Not too bad for a start, she thought. Reaching the last one- the easiest to remember since it consisted in joining the hands above the head, elbows in front, then dragging them down in six stages, holding back the breathing out, to last throughout the six stages- she was starting to feel that she was again losing contact with the ground. She did not dare look at her petits yiyis, but she was sure that she was a little higher than a few minutes before. She could hear them cicada-ing. Yes, she had initiated their speech, and was just beginning to control them, or at least to interact with them.

She landed softly, the cicada-ing ceased. She opened her eyes, they were still connected. Perhaps this is what they had been expecting, a little push from their owner. She would soon find out.

Chapter Five

Wednesday afternoon is usually time off for school-goers in France and pupils go to religious schools, dancing classes, sport clubs, or stay at home, since their parents are away earning a living- and in some cases, as in Pauline's building- the ladies managed their shifts so that one of them could look after the children including her own.

Pauline's father was the only single dad on the floor, out of twenty families. He often talked with the single mums, sometimes in languages that Pauline did not recognise, for instance with Judith, Sarah's mother.

"What is that language?" she had once asked, as her father bid goodbye to the lady, who was in her early thirties. "Hebrew," he replied. "I used to manage acceptably a long time ago, but now, without practice, I am a bit rusty but I still enjoy it."

Pauline put the answer in the corner of her mind and went back to the table, picked up the book she was reading and pretended to be content.

"Hum," her father said to himself, "I get away cheaply this time. I am glad she did not ask what I was doing in Israel long before I knew her mother. But one day, I shall have to tell her."

So, on that particular Wednesday, when Pauline's father was out on business and it was Judith's turn to look after the little gang, composed of Fatima, Nafissatou, Zhi Ruo, Pauline, and now Aurelio, in addition to her own Sarah, Pauline was eager to learn more.

"How come you speak with my father in Hebrew?" she had asked Judith. The young woman cleaned offices in a big building at night, but in the morning or afternoon, depending on her work schedule, she attended an art college, where she hoped to obtain a degree as a graphic designer for animation movies- a specialty where artists with a French diploma could find a job abroad. She spoke good French and even better English, so why use her own tongue, Pauline thought.

"It is good to converse in my mother language. I feel a bit home sick, and your father is so pleased to take a trip down memory lane." She saw that the little girl was uncertain of the meaning of the expression. "He still lives in the past, you know and when we speak Hebrew together, I can see that he relives scenes of some years ago."

As they were talking, Pauline saw that Sarah was sitting at the lounge table, scribbling funny characters, but right to left.

"What is that?"' she asked.

"These are Hebrew letters," Sarah replied. "I write each of them on a full line, just to get the hang of it."

Pauline was discovering their square shapes, impossible to guess. At least, when she spent vacations in Greece in her father's family, some letters were the same, even if they were not pronounced the same, but here, not a clue.

"How many letters do you have?"

"Twenty-two," she replied, "mostly consonants, you know, like "p", "b", "f", "m".

"You have no vowels, like a, o, i?" Pauline asked, intrigued.

"Only those with a long sound, like o as in door or ee as in sheep. Otherwise, we use little dots or dashes."

"It sounds very complicated!"

"But the verbs, the order of words, the grammar is much easier than French!"

Pauline remembered that her father told her how lucky she was to have been born to a French-German family, since both these languages were among the most difficult ones on the planet.

Pauline was following the gestures of Sarah on the paper. The Jewish girl was chewing her tongue as if to concentrate more.

"For us," Judith, her mother, stepped in, "these letters are holy. We say that they existed before the creation of the world. They are not only letters, you know, they are also words and symbols, and numbers."

That part sounded familiar, her Greek cousins had told her the same about the language of their ancestors.

"But, hang on a minute," she thought to herself, reliving the conversation she had had with her father a few days ago, when she asked about God. Her father had mentioned numbers as an element of God. She frowned, trying to understand. She had the impression of having pieces of a puzzle on the table and if she wanted to find the answers to her questions, she simply needed to put them together. As often, images and words were colliding in her brain. Here she was, with children like her, but from different parts of the world. Each had something in particular, perhaps none of them had the whole picture, perhaps they should team up to understand, like the separate letters, which were limited in power until they were grouped to form a word, and then to form a sentence.

The letters drawn by Sarah were not linked. She smiled, like a kind of code, and there she almost laughed, like the thousands of petits yiyis gathering at night, away from the presence of adults, from the real world. "Yes," she wondered, "this is only the beginning of my journey, of our journey."

***

"Look," Zhi Ruo said to Pauline, the following day, during the morning intermission. Once again Aurelio had to face the gang of bullies in the court yard. They seem to take turns, going from one lonely little boy to another. "They've got what it takes to become bankers or salesmen!" Nafissatou commented, tongue-in-cheek. "This is what my mum says when I tell her about them." Yes Pauline thought, it was all very well to day-dream, to study Hebrew letters, to discuss the nature of God with her father, to practice meditation Chi Qong and levitate with her petits yiyis vibrating more or less under her control, but there was a more pressing emergency: Aurelio, whose daily life was not a bed of roses. The five girls were tempted, once again, to rescue him, or at least to come between them, but they had already debated and decided that Aurelio would have to face them one day, on his own. On the other hand, he might be really discouraged and might even lose hope altogether if that day never came.

They needed to gain time. Fabien, with his blue eyes and blonde curly hair, strongly built for his age, was the leader. He was two years behind the others and would probably never be awarded the Nobel Prize of Medicine, but at the moment, he was the king of the school. Without his leadership, the other boys might leave Aurelio and the other victims alone.

Zhi Ruo knew that Fabien, although easily a couple of stones heavier than her, was no match for her in a fighting ring. She did not want to hurt him either, she did not want to stoop to his bullying level. Nonetheless, he needed to be taught a lesson. But how?

They had now finished with Aurelio, they had got the football trading cards or the few coins they had demanded and, as a reward, started to play with a ball.

Fatima, Sarah, Pauline, Nafissatou and Zhi Ruo exchanged glances in silence …

Judging by their game, the boys stood little chance of being recruited for Manchester United and the ball would inevitably get kicked out of the pitch drawn with a chalk at the far end of the court yard.

The girls moved slowly closer to them. As anticipated, one of the boys struck the ball too hard, which bounced on the goal post and out of the pitch. Meaning well Zhi Ruo took a few strides towards the ball, as if to save them the trip of leaving the pitch and bringing the ball back to the game. Still talking to her friends, while looking at Fabien from the corner of her eye, she kicked the ball, which met with Fabien's forehead. It was a violent blow, enough to make him stumble and fall onto his bottom.

"I am so sorry," Zhi Ruo exclaimed, running to his rescue. She arrived before his mates, grabbed his hand, firmly, and whispered into his ear. "If you don't stop bullying the little boys, I promise you, next time, I shall aim for your big fat nose!" Nobody had heard. He rose to his feet with difficulty, with shaking legs. Looking into the little Chinese girl's eyes, Fabien felt that although he could lift her with one arm, she meant what she had said. The other boys, laughing, caught the ball and resumed the game without him. He rested on a bench, out for the count.

"He doesn't look very happy!" Sarah said. Fabien was looking at the five girls, in disbelief. Were they actually challenging his power? How dare they? Anyway, that little Chinese girl would have to pay, some day.

"He's not going to become your best friend!" Fatima added, jokingly.

Aurelio had not seen what happened, which was just as well. Fabien could not take it out on him later.

"I think I'm now top of the list!" Zhi Ruo said. The girls had seen her practicing what she called forms, i.e. a set of movements, like the steps of a dance, in the corridor. She moved very fast and her blows in the air were fast and measured. They could not wait to see Fabien taunting her. But then again, would he be that stupid? All the more so, in front of his friends, at school?

"The good thing, for the time being, is that he might give the little boys a rest," she resumed, "but he won't stop."

***

After school and back to the corridor of the building where they lived, the girls and Aurelio discovered the next stage of the training given by Zhi Ruo. After the eighteen hand movements, she showed them the basic leg movements, very slowly, always breathing in and out in rhythm. Pauline started to feel her petits yiyis vibrating as she was moving. She prayed that she would not levitate in front of her friends. She was focussed on her moves and especially on calming down her petits yiyis, when she realised that her blows into the air were becoming more powerful. The more she concentrated, the more energy she could feel rising from her toes, feet, and legs, then her tummy, up into her arms and then down to her fingers, releasing the blows into an imaginary enemy- she could see the waves of air- like ripples at the surface of a lake. After a few moves like that, Zhi Ruo came up to her, slightly amazed. She put her left hand in front of Pauline. A few inches from where her right fist would reach. "Come on Pauline, push me!" Pauline breathed in, calling all the energy she could get from her petits yiyis, using her body as an amplifier, and breathed out, while slowly releasing the energy through her right fist. Zhi Ruo flinched briefly. Yes, she had felt something, or was she simply being kind, wanting to encourage her?

"Now, it's my turn," the Chinese girl said. "Extend your arm, present your palm to me and rest solidly on your feet. Look at the boards on the floor. Imagine they form a square. Place your feet on a diagonal, left foot first, close to me, right foot on the same diagonal, away from me. Your body facing me, firmly stable on your legs." She showed Pauline, "like that!" Her feet were placed on the diagonal of an imaginary square, the one at the back acting as a barrier in case the front one was forced to rise from the ground, like someone trying to keep a door shut while another person on the other side is pushing it.

"Ready?" Zhi Ruo asked. The other girls and Aurelio had stopped, to watch.

Pauline placed her feet on an imaginary diagonal line, held her arm at shoulder height, opened her palm towards Zhi Ruo and took a deep breath, inflating her tummy at the same time, feeling strong vibrations up and down her body. She nodded.

Zhi Ruo mimicked a tiger and moved towards Pauline, throwing a punch towards her palm. Instinctively, Pauline breathed out and as the punch stopped a few inches before her palm, she did not budge. She felt the waves of air bouncing back and saw Zhi Ruo as if in slow motion, also bouncing back. She smiled.

"I think you have the gift."

Chapter Six

In her dream, Pauline was on the island of Zakynthos where her father's cousin lived, a place famous for its olives, honey, wines and spices, an agricultural place, without any fumes from factories. Time seemed to have stopped there, thousands of years ago.

She was in an olive grove, halfway up in the mountain, with a lovely view of the deep blue sea. The wind from the shore was going from strength to strength and the sky was getting grey, with clouds turning into thunder. She hid under a big rock and could see the branches laden with olives shaking. The fruit started to fall, a few, then many, many, many. They seemed to dive into the water-drenched soil and disappeared from view.

After what felt an eternity, the storm ceased and the clouds vanished, leaving a beautiful rainbow and an immaculate blue sky.

Suddenly, Pauline could hear muffled sounds. She looked around, and unlike present times, there was not a single habitation to be seen, not a single road, not even a path; only dogs barking from higher up the mountain, and wild goats down below, grazing, without a shepherd, as if she had been catapulted to pre-historic days, before the dawn of man.

Leaves lying around started to fly away gently and rosy-yellow stems were shooting around the olive trees, where the fruit had fallen. The stems turned into chubby rainbows, multi-coloured sticks, no more than two centimetres in height, like vertical fat worms. Some had darker shades than others, and there were endless combinations. As minutes went by, they took a more graceful shape and started to slide onto the ground, then gradually rise into the air, softly, vibrating.

Some went back to the trees, crawling up the trunk, others were looking for a barren place, and seemed to sink into the ground as in quicksand, and, little by little, a stem would grow, turning into a young olive tree.

Pauline had the impression she was holding a camera with the fast-forward button depressed fully.

These little creatures looked very much like her petits yiyis. Some of them were playing, like acrobats, wrestling, jumping on top of each other, and stopping to form figures or letters in the air. These figures and letters would fly away, some fell into the sea, and others rose into the sky, giving birth to fish and birds.

After a moment, when a few new trees had reached a few centimetres, and after the younger, smaller, rainbow-like solid creatures had finished playing, groups began forming around the new trees. They began to vibrate, like cicadas, and the new trees were growing, growing, growing, with multitudes of olives appearing on their branches.

A few yiyis caught sight of Pauline. One of them bent forward, as if to beckon her, and made its way towards the little girl. Other petits yiyis followed. She left her hiding place and walked towards a clearing among the young trees. The little creatures surrounded her, and started to fly around in a circle, faster and faster. She closed her eyes. The first vision was that of two petits yiyis, one slightly taller and stronger-looking than the other, the other more delicate. They flew towards each other and landed on the field, sinking by a fraction of a centimetre into the soil, the wind pushed them against each other to form a single rainbow, interlaced, united, and then the rain started and they were struck by lightning.

They had vanished, in their stead, there was a little cocoon, changing shape as if something inside was trying to break out of the shell. The shell fell apart and a little creature, with human features, not quite transparent, like elongated drops with various shades of soft colours emerged. Pauline looked away and saw the rest of the field, with the same scene repeating itself, infinitely, countless cocoons turning into little rainbows.

Birds of prey gathered over the field, and collected hundreds of petits yiyis- before they could unite in twos under the four elements of nature, earth, wind, water and fire, some of rough shapes, others of more delicate appearance- and took them away, beyond the mountain, across the sea.

Images were accelerating and Pauline saw the little transparent rainbows growing, turning gradually into creatures that looked more and more human, with a head, and arms and legs pushing through the original drop shape, dancing joyfully around the trees by the sea, eating fruit and playing. Because they looked like drops of rain irradiating lights of different colours, Pauline decided to call them Rainlights. She could see them looking at the sky, with their hands outstretched, and others sitting with their legs under their bottoms, listening for the songs of birds and the sound of waves. Rain fell and they drank the drops. When the Rainlights grew older, the younger ones were kind and brought them fruit and water from the springs. When they were too weak, they sank into the ground and olive trees grew again, producing olives, which fell onto the ground and gave birth in turn, to countless petits yiyis, which gathered in twos in the fields - the cycle of life repeating itself.

Some Rainlights were living among olive groves and protected the petits yiyis from the birds of prey in the air and from bigger animals on the ground.

Sadly, she saw that some little Rainlights lost their brilliance and turned into angry and not so beautiful creatures. Pauline, decided to call them Angries. She could see them starting to fight with the Rainlights, stealing petits yiyis in the fields and apparently selling them to other angry creatures, to enslave them. The more the Angries fought with the Rainlights, the uglier and the greedier they were becoming, never having enough olive trees and petits yiyis.

The Rainlights hid in the mountains while the Angries built villages, then cities and roads. Some groups would stop and put fences around, and fight among themselves, then a group would leave, find another territory, grow in size, put up a fence, and the fight inside the tribe would start again, and again and again.

The territory of the Rainlights was getting smaller and smaller. They took refuge, where they could, in colder climates, in very hot climates, high in the mountains, and on remote islands, where the Angries were too lazy to chase them.

The Angries tried to wipe out the petits yiyis that had fallen from olive groves. Some wanted to destroy the original olive trees and plant new ones which would bear more fruit more quickly, and they would harvest them before they turned into petits yiyis, to prevent the birth of new Rainlights.

Without the Rainlights to look after them, the wild olive trees gradually ceased to produce petits yiyis, only wood, fruit and oil to the benefit of the Angries, who wanted to rule the world, without sharing it with the Rainlights.

Had they killed all the original trees? Was there one left?

Pauline woke up. Was it too late already? She looked at her petits yiyis. They seemed to be smiling.

***

For once, Pauline suggested the place for the Sunday outing, the Jardin des Plantes. As the name indicates it is a museum with plants, trees, and flowers from all over the world, like a library of what nature has to offer, from the most common to the rarest species. It is situated on the other side of the river Seine so Pauline and her father took a bus, where the view was far more pleasant than on the metro, with its endless tunnels.

As she was sitting opposite her father she wondered whether one day he would bring a woman home, to stay with them. She was in two minds: she missed the company of a loving mother but she was not in too much of a hurry to share her father with an intruder. At the moment she could speak to the mothers of her friends and, the girls, who had no father, could speak to her's, as if they all had part-time parents. Time would tell…

He signalled to her that they were approaching the stop.

The gardens were huge, with flowerbeds outside full of flowers with long names of Greek and Latin origin. The most fragile species were indoors.

There was even a Buddhist Temple on the right, at the end of an alley. She would ask him to go there some time, and perhaps they could make a day of it, with Zhi Ruo and her mother, and perhaps Nafissatou, Fatima, Sarah, Aurelio and their mothers. But right at that moment, Pauline had another project: she wanted to see, or rather to feel the presence of the trees, possibly of the rare trees, and ideally of the rare olive trees …

Unlike subjects like history or languages, nature was not her father's strongest point and she abstained from asking questions, knowing that he would not be able to answer.

They walked in silence among the flowerbeds, then entered the big greenhouse, filled with hundreds of trees from all around the world. Instantly, she felt as if a crowd were engrossed in a vivid conversation among villagers and stopped short, at the approach of a stranger in town.

She began to tremble slightly and pictures of her recent dream seemed to mingle with the trees, like two screens merging into each other.

Chapter Seven

« I have something important to tell you, » Pauline began. It was the following Monday. The five girls and Aurelio were gathered in the corridor, and as was now their custom, they had practiced Tai-Chi for twenty minutes. "Can we go to your place, Sarah?"

They all sat around the table and Pauline, humming and hawing began to tell them about her first strange night, when she had noticed the disappearance of her petits yiyis. She was speaking slowly, waiting for them to laugh at her, or pass comments which would have hurt her, but they didn't. Had they experienced something similar she wondered?

Zhi Ruo pointed out that she felt that Pauline indeed had some kind of power. Not a super power in the usual sense, like jumping on top of buildings, or moving cars just by extending one arm, as can be seen in many movies, but the ability to receive messages, like a sponge, from other worlds, perhaps from other periods in time.

Pauline continued with the description of her dream, pausing before mentioning that some petits yiyis were converted into Rainlights- who remained kind and protective of the trees and of nature- and others became Angries- who wanted to destroy the Rainlights, the original wild olive trees.

"So, you're saying that many people come from the Angries and only a few from the Rainlights? Nafissatou asked. Then she told them about many tales she had heard when she was on holiday in Cameroun, about long gone ancestors visiting the living to guide them- perhaps they were Rainlights?

Pauline then went on to describe her visit to the Jardin des Plantes, and the things she had learnt that the olive tree has represented for some civilisations- Goodness and Charity.

Finally she told them about her father's cousin, Giorgos, uncle Yorgi to her, who lived on the island of Zakynthos. None of the five children had heard of the little island, 20 x 80 km in size-in the shape of a hand with the thumb facing the four fingers- a little piece of land, planted between the South of Italy and the West of Greece, as if hiding from the rest of the world.

The five of them remained silent. Pauline was happy that nobody had made any jokes. They did not seem to think that she was crazy.

"Perhaps you have been chosen to do something?" Nafissatou wondered, looking at Pauline.

"Perhaps, but I don't know what. You are my friends, and you too, Aurelio. We must join forces." Pauline replied, wanting to include the new comer to their little club.

"As I understand," Fatima started, "the planet is dying, we can see this every day on television. The Angries- as you call them- are killing nature and turning wild trees into slaves. There may be more Rainlights somewhere but the Angries want to eliminate them all, and to do so, they need to destroy the few remaining wild olive trees"

"And there might be only one wild olive tree, still giving birth to what Pauline calls petits yiyis, it is a funny name," Sarah said.

"And if they find it, the planet can't be saved" Nafissatou added, with sadness in her voice.

"We must find the tree before they do!" Aurelio ventured, astonished at his courage at talking in front of the five girls.

"How do we start?" Pauline asked.

***

"Who are the Angries, and who are the Rainlights, how can they be recognised, where are they, what do they do?" Pauline wondered in the darkness of her bedroom after her father had left to entertain tourists, as he did every evening.

Perhaps the Angries are those who take and never give. She had often heard adults complaining about buying cars, computers, printers or mobiles which failed much sooner than promised. She had heard the same adults complaining about how difficult it was to get a loan from the bank and how much interest they had to pay on it. She could see in her mind a procession of her cousins, regardless of the country- France, Germany, Denmark or Greece- who often talked about the problems they encountered, but still managed to smile when they gathered at a table, with wine and plenty of food, and sometimes music, and forget for a while that life was not a bed of roses. Her cousins, she thought, her father, her friends at school, the ladies on the same floor did not come across as Angries, more like hopeful Rainlights, but not quite, as they looked very human.

Perhaps it was not that easy, and, like shades of a given colour, there was a whole range from very dark to very light. Perhaps people could sometimes be Angries and at other times closer to Rainlights.

Going back to her dream, the Angries wanted to eliminate all the wild olive trees that gave birth to petits yiyis, which in turn, with the help of the four elements of nature- earth, air, water and fire- gave birth to Rainlights. Some of the petit yiyis, in fact most of them, had turned into Angries, because they wanted more, all the time more, to the detriment of the other Rainlights who were just content to share what they had and spread joy and love.

She could ask her father for help, but felt she ought to find out a bit more on her own first. The bullies at school surely belong to the Angries category. As for the adults, it was not that easy to decide who was what. Then she had a light bulb moment: perhaps all children were born Rainlights, with hopes, smiles and dreams, then as they grew up, reality gradually destroyed their dreams, and made them sad. And those that were extremely sad wanted the others to be as sad as they were and even tried to spread greater sadness. She imagined people at the beginning of their lives being like perfect trees, but as they began to suffer, their leaves would turn into blades that they threw at each other, in a never-ending battle which nobody would ever win.

Now, she had some questions:- why did most of the Rainlights turn into Angries?

If the Angries wanted to wipe out all the wild olive trees, did they have a leader? Had they already found the last trees? How many pure olive trees were there and could Pauline and her friends find them before the Angries?

***

She was woken in the early hours of the morning by the return of her petits yiyis. They were normally silent, but this time, she could hear them whizzing around in the air, like little insects. As if this was not enough, they stopped on her desk where she usually did her homework and began to cicada. She could not see them clearly yet, but guessed that the ten of them were forming a circle before the flat screen of her computer.

A green ring of flying dust, like those around some planets, was rising from them, as if they had all lit a match and the little flames were joining each other. There was no danger, it was only green dust spots growing into a whirl pool just above the petit yiyis, perhaps almost a metre in height and small at the root, widening up to thirty centimetres in diameter. She had the impression that a shape was inside, with human features. She wiped her eyes with her fists gently, wondering whether she was dreaming again.

She could see long blonde hair inside the green whirl pool and green eyes.

"Mutti!" she exclaimed, with tears in her eyes.

"Wie geht's Dir, mein Schatz?" (How are you, my darling), Pauline believed she heard.

She leapt from the bed and hopped to her table. Her mother's head seemed to be floating inside the green whirl pool. Had she become a Rainlight again?

"I have never left you," her mother went on to say. "But sadly, you could not see me or perhaps I did not have the power to make you see me. It seems to work now, at last."

Pauline extended her hand through the whirl pool and it went through her mother's features. She felt the moisture of drops around her fingers, but the light did not disappear.

"I may not be able to stay very long, you know, but this is a nice beginning," her mother added with a smile.

"Will you come back?" Pauline asked, afraid.

"Of course, but you must help me. We can only appear to those who are pure at heart."

"What can I do if I want to talk to you?" Then she thought of a better question: "Can you come back for good, as before?"

"No, not as before ..." Pauline had the impression that her mother was silenced by another presence, but was not sure. "But we shall be united again one day, in a different way, trust me."

Pauline wanted this moment to last and last ...

"Don't cry, I am not in pain. I see you all the time, but we can't do as we wish, there is so much sorrow to comfort. We must take turns"

Who was this "we"? Pauline thought.

"If you want to talk to me, just let what your father calls your petits yiyis guide you. They are the go-betweens between the different worlds."

The green whirl pool around Pauline's mother rose almost to the ceiling and she could now make out the whole figure of her mother, clothed in a kind of chiffon, ruffled dress.

She climbed onto her desk, and craned her neck to look into her mother's eyes.

She would have loved so much to be held in her arms, as in the past. She closed her eyes, feeling that it would be time for goodbye, soon.

"Can I come into the green circle?" she asked.

"One day, but be patient."

Then she saw her mother kneel and press softly against the sides of the green whirl pool. She felt wet fingertips on her cheeks, then a fleeting kiss. In tears, she grabbed her mother's hands for a few seconds. She released her grip and her mother stood up, went back into the green circle, blew a kiss and vanished.

She climbed down onto the floor, slightly unbalanced without her petits yiyis.

The green whirl pool seemed to be deflating and absorbed back into the ten little creatures who then went back to their usual mooring places.

Now Pauline had even more questions to ask than the day before.

Chapter Eight

The following morning, Pauline hesitated: should she tell her father that she spoken to her mother, eighteen months after her fatal accident? No, she wanted to wait for another meeting, before she told him.

She was beginning to realise how awesome their task was, to find and save the last wild olive tree. Why them? Probably, going by what her mother had said, because one needed to be pure in mind and humble in spirit.

During the intermission in school, she called a short gathering with the other 5 members of the Rainlights fan club.

"How can we know whether the Angries are close to their goal?" she began.

"We can't put an ad on a blog reading "we want to save the last olive tree and protect the planet. If you know where it is, please private message me!" Fatima ventured and they all laughed.

"We need to keep quiet, and undetected…" Nafissatou commented.

"The olive tree comes originally from the Middle-East, but the legends diverge as to the exact location, but this narrows down our research to more or less the size of France, over a dozen countries, on strips close to the shore."

"We can't ask our parents to treat us to a few years' holiday on our own in the sun either!" Aurelio contributed, visibly gaining in self-confidence.

"On the other hand," Pauline commented, "we all have cousins or grand-parents around Spain, the South of France, Italy, Greece, the Middle-East and North-Africa, and I've discovered from the Internet that olive trees have been planted more and more in China, so we can split the search in six parts." They all nodded, rummaging in their brains and putting faces to places, an uncle there, a second cousin in another place and so on, but the summer, the ideal moment to stay there for a few weeks, was still 7-8 months away.

"Another possibility," Sarah stepped in, winning their full attention, "we could tackle the problem from the other end." Their stunned eyes encouraged her to continue. "If we knew who a person or a group of people is, or are on that quest, we could simply shadow him, her or them and try to arrive first."

There was a little pause. This sounded like a cunning plan alright.

"Yes, that is a wonderful idea," Fatima said, "providing we make sure that we follow the right person, not a decoy, to lead us astray and waste precious time."

"What do you say, Pauline?" Zhi Ruo asked, looking at a very thoughtful Pauline.

"We did not know anything about the Rainlights and the Angries until a couple of weeks ago. Perhaps we have been chosen, not at random, but as part of plan, a design. Perhaps there are…. people, I don't know what to call them, somewhere. Perhaps we must prove ourselves to them in one way or another, and only then will they help us."

***

Pauline thought that what the six of them needed, was a decisive breakthrough, something to bond them closer together.

Caution was the word. Pauline had invited her five friends to her flat after her father left, hoping that something would happen before Sarah's mother, Judith, looked in on her.

They tip-toed into her flat in silence. Pauline asked them to remove their slippers, to form a circle and to join hands. She closed her eyes and focussed gently, feeling the assistance of Zhi Ruo, Sarah, Nafissatou and Fatima. Aurelio still had some work to do, but he gradually felt the energy of the group passing from one to the next, in a clockwise motion, like a flame lighting a candle, then landing on the next, jumping onto the next, and so on, each time gaining in strength.

They were all firmly on their feet. The sound of the cicadas increased. Their toes were trembling and suddenly they took off, like a plane on a runway, taxiing slowly, then suddenly switching into a faster gear. Pauline felt a little ripple of fright from her friends.

All of them could visualise their petit yiyis going up the wall, past the skylight, and flying like the Milky Way, as if propelled by the six young friends, gaining strength, as well as speed, above the roof tops of Paris, like a squadron of reconnaissance aircrafts.

They landed outside the building where Pauline had followed them the first time.

The room was full as the time before, but, this time, the blasting entrance of sixty petits yiyis caused those waiting to become agitated, like a hangar where lights were being switched on from one end to the other. They all started to glow, turning into little Rainlights as if they had been asleep or sad, and now, hope was breathed into them. Perhaps they had been hiding there, waiting for a message or a messenger.

The sixty petits yiyis were flying over those who waited, brushing past all of them, as if to greet them and hug them, as if they were Refugees abandoned by their companions.

They were still glowing with multiple colours when the squadron bid them goodbye and flew back to Pauline's flat.

The sixty toes reconnected without hesitation to their respective owners. Pauline was smiling inwardly. Wouldn't it be funny if they all had an assortment of petits yiyis, slightly yellow from Zhi Ruo, white-pink from Pauline, coffee with milk from Fatima, black from Nafissatou, tanned from Aurelio and pale tan from Sarah.

Once their feet were again in walking order, the field of energy slowed down and left them. They let go of each other's hands and looked at each other, glowing with the feeling of having accomplished something. They did not know exactly what, but obviously, what Pauline had told them was not a fairy tale.

"We must find a better hiding place for the little Refugees!" Fatima said.

"God knows how long they have been in hiding..." Sarah added.

"Yes, we have a mission," Zhi Ruo whispered.

***

After making sure that nobody was in the corridor, they all left, lost in their thoughts.

Where could the little Refugees be taken? Pauline was wondering, alone in her father's flat. They had belonged to someone, where were their owners now? Dead? In another world? Or had they sacrificed themselves, leaving their petits yiyis behind like seeds for future generations?

Pauline imagined asking her father to rent a truck, load the little Refugees and take them to the sun, to his cousin's island, where they could resume their lives. But he might think she was going round the bend!

Pauline and her friends had to find them a secure place, a sunny place, away from war, the choice was becoming more and more limited, thanks to the Angries.

Actually, why find only one place? That might make them too easy to find.

Perhaps they were the last batch of the past. Why were they hiding in Paris? What would have happened if her mother had not been killed? As it was only after that when her father decided to leave the mountains near Switzerland and go back to his roots, and live in the French capital. Was it all pure coincidence? Was there a pattern?

***

Pauline's father would never let her take the metro on her own. He would send her out to the baker's for a baguette, or to the charcutier for saucisson and pâté occasionally, but so far, he was adamant: either she was accompanied by one of the ladies on the top floor, by himself, or a group of more than 4 children. Not that Paris was a war zone', but, simply, he was worried that she might meet the wrong person.

She was pleased to tell him that she enjoyed her training with Zhi Ruo and the rest of her gang. He showed her a few basic defence moves, probably memories from his childhood in the Chinese monastery.

"One step at a time," he had said when she asked for more information. "Everything comes when you really need it."

Right now, they were on a bus. Lifting her gaze from the streets of Paris, her attention was caught by pictures above the heads of the other passengers. Pauline had not focussed on anything in particular she was just wondering about the Angries.

There was a middle-aged man on the other side of the bus, by the window, looking sad, the total opposite of the little boy that he had once been, she could see him playing joyfully with a football, like a hologram above his head, like a souvenir still lingering in his memory.

There was a woman, with a little girl sitting opposite her, a little older than Pauline. The woman was playing with vials containing liquids, mixing them and obtaining fumes from a beaker, she was in a laboratory, as an adolescent. Then, as if in fast-forward motion on a computer screen, she could see the woman with a baby alone in a small room, and finally at a check-out in a supermarket, her dreams of becoming a scientist destroyed.

Pauline was going from one face to another, every time she could see people's past dreams, and now their quiet resignation. Some looked more spiteful than others, as if willing to fight and to inflict pain on those around them. She had the feeling that for some, it would not take much for them to give way to hatred and actually enjoy being spiteful and violent.

She had a hunch, perhaps most people, after a certain age, turned into Angries. Perhaps they were not organised, although, she had heard of battles in the past where millions of people had killed millions of others, so someone must have had the power, the genius to rally their hatred against a common target.

No, people were not born Angries, it seemed to be the standard course of nature, for most of them.

Were there still Rainlights among the world of adults, how many were there and could she and her friends trust them?

If there was no structure, no army of Angries as such, no easily identifiable enemy, it was even more frightening …

Chapter Nine

Christmas would soon be round the corner and the yiyis Refugees might suffer from the cold in their basement. Pauline was not a yiyi-doctor, but looking at hers and her friends' and comparing them with those gathered in the dark, she concluded that they did not seem as healthy. How long could they stay there?

She decided to call a meeting with her friends after school and their Tai-Chi training, before doing their homework, especially before any adult might interrupt their brainstorming session.

"We must answer three questions, at least:-where to take them, how to take them there and what they need to survive, in terms of … well … power supply."

The four other girls and the boy set their grey cells in motion.

"Would they be strong enough to be towed in the air by our own sixty petits yiyis?" Aurelio ventured. "We all know that it has to be kept secret and the only way of getting a truck or a van would involve that we ask one of our parents …"

"We could use wheelbarrows at night, cover them with a blanket and bring them to a place of safety," Fatima added. "Providing it is not too far- but there again, six kids pushing wheelbarrows through the winter streets of Paris might look strange…" She observed with a smile.

"We must find a warm place, secluded from the public, so, not a shop, or a train station, or a metro station ..." Sarah thought aloud.

"Wait a minute," Pauline stepped in, "a warm place? Yes I've got it, a green house, a big greenhouse, a tree nursery..."

"You mean a garden centre? But we said that it needed to be closed to public access..." Zhi Ruo commented.

"Absolutely," Pauline replied. "I was thinking of the Jardin des Plantes. You know, the huge museum of natural sciences in Paris. There are thousands of trees and species of vegetables and plants. There is a dedicated staff who look after them and there are places reserved for scientists and researchers only, closed to the public."

They all remained silent for a while, weighing the pros and cons.

"If it is closed to the public, how do we get in there? Let alone, at night? How do we bring the Refugees? How can we visit them later?" Nafissatou bombarded them with questions.

"Either we get an adult, or several adults in the loop, or we find help on the inside" Sarah said.

The children were not too enthusiastic about sharing their adventure with an adult, who-and it was a risk not to be brushed aside lightly- might turn into an Angry and betray them.

"I like your idea of the Jardin des Plantes," Fatima uttered, "perhaps we could have a reconnaissance trip with our petits yiyis, one night."

***

61

They had all set their alarm clock for midnight, the best time, after a few mothers had gone to work and before the others came back. Also the traffic was not as busy as in the day or before 5 o'clock, when Paris would wake up again, with trucks, motorbikes, garbage collectors and hooting klaxons from impatient drivers.

Sarah had printed a map of Paris, with various itineraries from the Sacré-Coeur, where they would get their initial bearing. For the Great Move, they would need to take the Refugees a few streets away, to the heart of Montmartre, not far from the Moulin-Rouge.

They were scrutinising the map laid on the table. As the crow flies, or in this case as the petits yiyis fly, the distance to the Jardin des Plantes was about 6 km. They had no idea how fast they could travel, but they estimated that a few minutes should suffice.

"How high would they fly?" Aurelio asked.

"We need to keep it simple," Sarah replied, "and avoid districts with sky-scrapers. The easiest way would be to fly over a boulevard or large avenues, down to the river Seine, and then turn left, towards Notre-Dame Cathedral, with the Tour Eiffel behind us, as a beacon. When we arrive at the Cathedral, we will continue for three kilometres and the Jardin des Plantes is on our right." She had been pointing at the map with her right index finger to show the route. The plan sounded reasonable.

"But when we arrive over the flowerbeds and the various buildings, where do we go then?" Nafissatou wondered, bent over the map.

Sarah had printed a map of the Museum, which was as big as at least 35 Olympic swimming-pools.

"When you go on the website," Pauline started, "they give you the details of where things are, animals, vegetables, trees, the temperature, etc."

"When you look at the building marked "E", you discover that one of the greenhouses is a tropical greenhouse..." Sarah said. Both girls had done their homework and did not want to leave too much to chance.

"The atmosphere is warm and humid, ideal for petits yiyis in poor health," Zhi Ruo commented.

Now came the great moment, would it work, they all seemed to wonder.

They removed their slippers and socks.

"Let's hope that our petits yiyis have not decided to call a strike!" Aurelio exclaimed.

Pauline climbed on her desk and lifted the skylight slightly, then returned to her friends.

She was setting the pace. She waited for Sarah to take her left hand, then clockwise, Fatima, Zhi Ruo, Nafissatou and finally Aurelio taking Pauline's right hand.

They all closed their eyes, summoning their petits yiyis. They could soon sense the cicadas. Now came the time of truth: the first time, they followed in mind the air travel of their petits yiyis, but now, they wanted to drive them. It was a different kettle of fish.

They started to breathe regularly, as Zhi Ruo had taught them during their few Chi-Qong lessons. Pauline was the first to feel her petits yiyis leaving her feet, it was then Sarah's turn, Fatima's, Zhi Ruo's, Nafissatou's and Aurelio's, to complete the squadron.

They left the flat through the skylight, then paused above the roof tiles, as if waiting for ground control to give flight directions.

As if playing a video game, the six children tilted their heads to accompany the movements of their petits yiyis, using their heads like joysticks.

Pauline's were leading, rather like a V-shaped squadron, followed by those of the other members of this reconnaissance trip, all in a V-shaped pattern.

It felt as if each of the six was propelled and/or towed by the other five.

Within seconds, they were flying above the Moulin-Rouge. Pauline relaxed, knowing that it was going to be a few minutes at least before they reached the Jardin des Plantes, and they all needed to save their strength.

Then they headed southward, using the Tour Eiffel as a beacon, veered left over the River Seine, accelerated towards Notre-Dame and started their descent procedure. They were hovering above the Jardin des Plantes. It seemed that the trip had taken 3 – 4 minutes, which would have been completely impossible on the ground with a car or even a motorbike.

Pauline could make out the greenhouse two thirds of the way up the main path of the garden.

Now, another tricky bit: how to enter the tropical greenhouse?

"Use your brain!" she thought to herself, "quickly!" The greenhouse needed some kind of ventilation, air drawn from outside, then heated and injected into the greenhouse.

"But hang on," she said to herself, "if they use a compressor, there might be blades or some kind of rotary mechanism that will shred our petits yiyis..."

Air had to be evacuated as well, but entering that way, through the exit, would mean fighting against pressure, and the petits yiyis might be projected by the force and knocked out for the count, on the grounds of the garden, on that cold winter night.

Another possibility was to dive into a pane of glass, ideally one that was not too thick and easier to break through. The hole in the glass did not need to be big, but perhaps the petits yiyis were not strong enough to drill through a glass pane. Also that would be forced entry, like burglary, so Pauline decided against it.

"Let's all focus," she said aloud. "We are going to hover, forming a fan- me on the left then, in succession, with Aurelio on the far right- in front of the big gate, in the centre of the building."

She could feel the level of energy rising in the circle they formed in the room, while they saw in their minds their petits yiyis forming a fan-pattern, with the cicadas growing from strength to strength. The lock in the door opened as the cicadas grew louder and a batten of the gate moved slightly on its hinges, only a few centimetres, but enough for the 6 V-shaped squadrons to fly into the tropical greenhouse.

Pauline hesitated. Should they let the petits yiyis rest for a while on the moist soil around the trees, if they did that the children might need extra energy to help them take off again. They were hovering a few inches above the ground, slowly, feeling the branches shivering as they moved between them. There were a few radiators to diffuse heat and their glowing red lights helped Pauline take her bearings.

"Let's go home, my friends!" she whispered. Her petits yiyis led the way back to the gate. They stopped, forming the same fan-shape, brought the batten back in contact with the other, and activated the lock.

As if to test their abilities, once they were above the River Seine, Pauline accelerated, went straight on, then veered gently towards the Tour Eiffel. "Trust me," she exclaimed, feeling stronger than ever. The six Vs arrived at the foot of the big tower, then as a game she started to circle around it, higher and higher, faster and faster, then, when they were all 300 metres above the ground- the height of the tower-she turned right towards the Moulin-Rouge.

Within seconds, the petits yiyis flew back through the skylight and reconnected with their owners.

The children opened their eyes, mesmerised. The petits yiyis looked happy, as if this night trip had been what they had always been looking for, a bit of adventure, but with a mission, mixing business and pleasure.

They didn't feel tired.

"Now," Zhi Ruo ventured, "can we tow thousands of petits yiyis?"

"We may have to make several trips ..." Fatima answered.

"And then, where do we put them?" Aurelio wondered, guessing the reply, within a fraction of a second.

"We plant them in the soil, around the tropical trees..." Pauline stated matter of factly.

"But we need far more training." Zhi Ruo said, looking at her friends. Indeed, the pilots appeared more tired than their petits yiyis!

Chapter Ten

« Someone has not been very cautious, apparently … » Pauline's father said, watching early morning TV while she enjoyed her breakfast, pretending not to understand the extent of the damage.

A couple of Japanese tourists on their honeymoon were being interviewed. They had dined the night before in the Jules Verne restaurant, one of the most expensive ones in Paris and one of the best in the world, with its 6 course tasting menu, each with a great vintage wine. Her father had taken her mother there for a romantic dinner, the year before she was born. But today, the atmosphere was not so joyful.

The Japanese claimed they saw a flock of what looked like flageolet beans, arranged as a succession of Vs, flying behind each other, close to the window, just as the man and the woman were choosing their next destination. They could not believe their eyes and thought that they were victims of drinking too much wine which they were unaccustomed to.

There were other witnesses too, a group of American businessmen. They were celebrating another victory for their bank, when the guy who was giving the "thank you all toast" stopped short as he saw a flock of what he described as small pork sausages, flying around the restaurant. He admitted that they were all pretty drunk by that time, half past midnight, but nevertheless, something was wrong. A prank, from young students from an engineering school, with miniature drones, trying to frighten tourists, after losing a challenge with their fellow students perhaps.

If something of the sort had happened in a little village in the mountains, it would have gone unnoticed, but not in Paris, at one of the most visited monuments on the planet!

She did not want to catch her father's eye. Did he suspect anything? Did he too talk to her mother? For the time being she needed to consult with her friends. Things were not progressing as planned...

***

"Well, so much for discretion..." Zhi Ruo said in the courtyard.

"There is no time to waste now!" Aurelio said, because we don't know who the Angries are, we suspect that some are worse than others and probably want to destroy the Refugees.

"They don't know where the Refugees are, otherwise they would have eradicated them already!" Fatima said.

"Unless they know that someone, like us, will try to save the Refugees and they are waiting for us to get them out and then they will attack" Sarah stated.

"They simply need to lie in waiting by the River Seine, close to the Tour Eiffel ..." Nafissatou added.

"It makes our task more complicated," Zhi Ruo intervened, "but think of what Kung-Fu tells us: turn a disadvantage into an advantage and use the opponent as a prop, not an obstacle."

They could not wait to see what she meant exactly

***

Before the Great Move, a few questions remained: would the Refugees have enough strength to fly the 6 km or so to the tropical greenhouse in the Jardin des Plantes, could they do it on their own or would they need to be towed? Would they need all six children's yiyis for the whole batch, and could Pauline and Zhi Ruo, who were apparently the strongest, take more than the other four children or should both of them concentrate on the weakest of the Refugees? How could the children determine the level of energy in each Refugee?

Sadly, the episode at the Tour Eiffel, with tourists having witnessed UFPYs (Unidentified Flying Petits Yiyis), did not allow time for a carefully thought-through course of action.

So, that evening, they decided to take a few short-cuts.

They assembled in Pauline's flat and removed their slippers, Pauline opened the skylight and they joined hands. This time, no fooling around, straight to the point. They sent their petits yiyis directly to the basement.

The Refugees were cicada-ing with joy as the six groups of ten petits yiyis mingled with them. Pauline felt it was a little like visiting a kennel of rescued dogs all needing a home.

She and her friends would have to make choices. How many Refugees were there, hundreds, thousands and how old were they?

"Let's try to raise them all off the ground," Pauline said, "but if we feel the load becoming too heavy we stop."

The children could feel huge waves of air, like a chopper taking off vertically.

"Are we all fit to continue?" She asked.

"Yes," the other five friends replied.

"Let's go for it, then!"

The six children took a deep breath and the six groups of petits yiyis adopted a typical Air Force formation: the leader at the front, two protectors on each side and a watchman at the back- in this case Zhi Ruo's petits yiyis.

They all flew away from the basement. The strongest Refugees were scattered along the outer side, with the weakest in the middle, so that they could be sucked in and pushed forward by the more able-bodied.

The Tour Eiffel was in sight within a few seconds. Pauline and her friends had switched into the fastest possible gear and the plan was make or break. They did not fly around it, as the night before, but turned left, hovering above the River Seine. The whole bunch was the size of a basket-ball ground, with the petits yiyis carefully spaced so that they did not to bump into each other and also to utilise the waves of air created by the strongest to help them along.

They were soon in sight of Notre-Dame Cathedral. However their speed was decreasing. Pauline and Zhi Ruo felt that their four companions were getting exhausted, and the petits yiyis in the middle seem to weigh tons. But that was not all, a cloud of smoke was following them very quickly. Zhi Ruo's petits yiyis at the back of the flying squadron started to cough. The cloud was closing in on them, and gradually, all the petits yiyis began to have headaches, as if they were inhaling toxic fumes from a chemical factory. Even the children in Pauline's gang were beginning to cough.

"Mutti," Pauline called in her head, "Hilfe (help me)" She felt the presence of her mother and said, "Sarah and Fatima, you take the lead, Nafissatou and Aurelio you guard the back. Zhi Ruo, you and I will stay behind, as a decoy, trust me, we don't have much time."

They were only a few hundred metres away, and the four children- assisted by the strongest of the petits yiyis- made a crash landing on the flower beds, away from the sight of the toxic cloud.

Pauline's and Zhi Ruo's petits yiyis remained at the level of Notre-Dame Cathedral, in a cluster, rubbing the ends of their toes together- as scouts do with flint stones- to create sparks. The sparks were tiny at first, but the two girls breathed in as much air as they could- filling up their stomachs, as they did during their Chi-Qong training- and expelled it as forcefully as they could towards the toxic cloud. A spark like a spearhead hit the cloud as it was about to absorb them, causing a big flash of lightning, the flash projected Pauline's and Zhi Ruo's petits yiyis a few dozen metres back.

They regrouped and rubbed against each other to create another gigantic spark that hit the cloud a second time, at the same place as the first one. The cloud split up- falling into pieces, like a jigsaw puzzle thrown out of a window-and the stench this generated was appalling.

The two girls felt the debris, like shards of glass launched at them, and each of them contained a face filled with hatred.

The shards split into tiny fragments and fell into the River Seine.

Pauline's and Zhi Ruo's petits yiyis joined the rest of the patrol.

Nafissatou and Fatima's petits yiyis were acting like nurses in a war zone, taking the healthier Refugees into the tropical greenhouse and digging little holes like beds for them.

Sarah and Aurelio's had remained with the more exhausted. They were all elated at the sight of Pauline and Zhi Ruo's groups.

Some of the Refugees had to be helped one by one to the tropical greenhouse.

After a few minutes, all the Refugees had found a new home. The younger ones soon regained energy quickly- like a plant watered at last after a couple of weeks of neglect - and were soon standing up proudly like straight stems.

Others were doing their best, putting on a brave face, and extending upwards painstakingly.

Sadly, a few looked really down on their luck. One of them, old and wrinkled, seemed to motion Pauline's petits yiyis to come closer. It could not cicada very loudly, but what Pauline could understand was frightening.

***

Pauline and her friends were in her room, but their petits yiyis stayed in the Jardin des Plantes. The children were exhausted. "We need a little rest, we can't risk racing against another cloud of Angries yet!' Sarah said.

The trip had lasted close to one hour, much longer than their previous trips, and they had no idea whether the petits yiyis needed refuelling, like themselves.

Pauline saw images in her mind of when she had called her mother for help when they were being chased by the cloud of angry stinking faces.

"Yes, it could be fun!" she said aloud.

"What have you got in mind?' Zhi Ruo asked, hoping that her idea wouldn't involve too much physical effort.

"We are going to play tourist" Pauline replied.

The Jardin des Plantes is by the River Seine, so they waited for a Bateau-Mouche (ferry boats offering dining, with champagne and accordion music, that go up and down the river) then they simply flew across the road and the bank and landed on top of the captain's cabin.

A few minutes later, past the Musée du Louvres- where Pauline had been a couple of weeks before with her father- they disembarked at the Place de la Concorde, at the foot of the Champs -Elysées, flew a hundred metres then waited in a bush in the Jardin des Tuileries.

"Let's wait for the number 30 bus, it will take us directly to the Moulin-Rouge, in about 20 minutes" Pauline said. She realised just how useful it had been to travel around Paris with her father, by bus.

Chapter Eleven

It has been a close call. Pauline assumed that their 'joy-flying' around the Tour Eiffel had attracted the attention of the Angries who had simply waited for them at a strategic point. She could remember the cloud chasing them, and, thanks to her mother's help, she and Zhi Ruo had been able to react swiftly, rubbing their petits yiyis together like flints, throwing sparks at the cloud and turning it into shards of glass with angry faces inside.

What was she supposed to make of it? The wrinkled old petit yiyi that had spoken to her in the Jardin des Plantes had shed some light on the matter, but she still had questions:-Where did the cloud come from, and was it activated by someone or several people? What did it want, to capture them, kill them, or turn them into who knows what?

Perhaps it was time to have a conversation with her mother.

She was alone in her room, the other children had recovered their petits yiyis and gone to bed.

She thought that hers had had enough and did not want to call upon them again to help contact her mother.

She closed her eyes and thought of her, gently, brushing aside any other images. Gradually, she felt a little draught a few feet away in front of her. She opened her eyes and the green whirl pool seemed to take root from her petits yiyis, who were sound asleep. The green form seemed to be connected to them, like rope linking an astronaut to his rocket in space.

As the green form rotated and expanded from Pauline's petits yiyis towards the ceiling, her mother's features started to appear, fading and then clearing, as a programmer plays with a mouse to adjust the picture on a screen.

When her mother's face seemed to settle in the middle of the green whirl pool, Pauline smiled.

"Thank you Mutti, without your help, I don't know what would have happened."

"What did you learn tonight, mein Schatz (my darling), from the old petit yiyi?"

This was the moment that Pauline had been waiting for.

"Well, he said that there were hiding places, all over the world, for forgotten petits yiyis."

"Did he say why?"

"I'm not sure that I understand this part, he said that they are like milk teeth, or in this case milk petits yiyis, that are left to rot and replaced by wisdom toes, but not in everybody's case."

'That's right. The milk petits yiyis fall when dreams, hopes, innocence and kindness start to decline. In certain children, sometimes later in life, they are pushed away one night by wisdom toes and, then most of the time, the Rainlights send special teams of pure petits yiyis to collect the milk ones. They take them to safety in the hope that one day, they can grow again, as at the beginning of Humanity before the Angries started to spread over the whole universe."

"Why did you say that **most of the time** the Rainlights send a sort of rescue squad, why not always?"

"It is a question of manpower, the Rainlights are becoming fewer and fewer and the Angries are increasing in number

Pauline was trying to figure it all out. The olive trees produced olives, they fell into the ground, gave birth to pure petits yiyis, who in turn produced Rainlights, but, sadly many of them turned into Angries. Children were born with a portion of Rainlight attached to them- their milk petits yiyis-and some of them remained kind and full of love, but many became bullies and greedy. They lost their milk petits yiyis and grew wisdom toes, which ought to be called hate-filled toes, not wisdom toes, because instead of being connected to goodness and innocence , they became connected to selfishness and betrayal, just like someone taking his car to a petrol station and choosing to fill the tank with diesel or regular.

She explained all that to her mother. It was a lot to take in, but she got the gist of it. "So, do all children become Angries? She asked, worriedly.

"No," her mother answered, "But far too many."

"Am I a Rainlight? Or am I connected to a Rainlight?" she continued, filled with expectations. "What about Nafissatou, Zhi Ruo, Fatima, Sarah and Aurelio?"

"Yes, all of you are connected to the Rainlights and it is your choice, and YOUR choice only to remain so."

***

The following day, in the afternoon, Pauline found herself again with her friends, this time she told them about her conversation with the wrinkled old petit yiyi, and about what her mother had told her.

It began to make sense, there were still many loose ends, but one step at a time.

"How can we get in contact with the other Rainlights?" asked Nafissatou, rather pleased that they could be called that.

"We could use the Internet, every child has access to a computer and we all know how to use networks, firewalls and what not," Aurelio ventured to say.

"The snag is", Sarah interrupted, "that many of them are also extremely good hackers. Look at the CIA, or any Intelligence service in the world, any skilled hacker can get the address of a general's dentist, or the bank statement of a head of state!"

They all laughed.

"No, we need to go back to the basics," Zhi Ruo thought aloud. "The Internet has only been around for a few decades, so how did the Rainlights protect their own against the Angries in the past?"

"According to what you've told us," Fatima commented, looking at Pauline, "there are countless abandoned petits yiyis all over the planet. Can you imagine them left alone in scorching deserts, rapids, rainforests or in freezing cold mountains?"

Indeed, they were building pictures of petits yiyis covered in sand, chased by scorpions, crocodiles, and hawks, or frozen into snowmen, rejected like broken toys on smoking bonfires.

"There must be clues, some signs somewhere, left for the Rainlights but unnoticeable to the Angries, that only those in the know would recognise," said Sarah.

"That's the point" Pauline thought aloud. "We need to be initiated into the Secrets of the Rainlights, to learn to decipher what is around us and take it from there."

"You're right," Nafissatou continued, "Perhaps this first trip was a test. Perhaps some Initiates wanted to make sure that they could entrust us with their knowledge." She could remember so many tales her grandparents told of young children having to prove their courage to the village before being accepted among the world of adults. In fact, each of them could remember their elders telling similar stories. They started to tell the stories which they had heard during holidays with their families in Portugal and Brazil for Aurelio, Algeria for Fatima, Cameroon for Nafissatou, China for Zhi Ruo, Israel for Sarah and Greece, Germany and Denmark for Pauline.

They were all different but yet so similar. In all their cultures, there were always assemblies of elders- sometimes men, sometimes women- trying to preserve the Tradition, the beliefs that held a group together. It was as if these assemblies were connected to the Rainlights and resisted the clouds composed of stinking hate-filled faces, as sharp as shards of glass.

"Back to reality," Pauline said all of a sudden, "we need to make sure that the Refugees have not been attacked. Anyone game for a little night trip?"

'Shall we take the bateau-mouche and the number 30 bus again on the way back?" Aurelio asked, jokingly.

They assumed the usual take-off position, but this time they headed North of Paris, followed the North Circular-an easy task, since it is like a belt, with four lanes, sometimes six- then as the sort of motorway crossed the River Seine in the East, by the Bois de Vincennes, (a little like Hyde Park in London or Central Park in New York), they veered right, followed the river from the opposite direction to the one they had previously, to avoid flying by the Tour Eiffel, and landed in the Jardin des Plantes.

Zhi Ruo and Pauline's petits yiyis stayed behind, to keep watch, just in case, while the other children's petit yiyis flew quietly to the tropical greenhouse.

As they entered it was as if someone had pressed a switch and lights came on where the Refugees had been planted. Some were shining more powerfully than others and a few were barely flashing, like bulbs running out of energy.

"How can we feed them?" Nafissatou asked.

"We can't go to a local shop and ask for special food for petits yiyis" Aurelio answered, laughing.

"I have an idea!" Fatima said. 'Let's stroke them. Remember what Pauline told us about kindness and love."

They sent their petits yiyis to hug the Refugees in less healthy condition and it seemed to work. The four children were regaining hope when Zhi Ruo's petits yiyis barged into the tropical greenhouse.

"Quick, get out, the cloud is back!"

They all gathered around Pauline's petits yiyis. They could not see the cloud, but the stench was getting stronger. They rose above the Jardin des Plantes, hiding behind the top of the roof of the main building and saw half a dozen clouds patrolling over the River Seine. The Refugees were safe, but for how long?

"We need to lead them away from here," Pauline said. "Follow me!"

The sixty petits yiyis formed the battle squadron of six Vs, with Pauline's leading and Zhi Ruo's last. They came out of hiding and flew briefly over the River Seine, to attract the attention of the clouds of Angries, judging by terrible stench they generated, their name was most suitable.

The Clouds noticed them and the chase began at once.

Pauline veered right towards the Bois de Vincennes, this was the first part of her plan.

As they arrived close to the woods, they started to fly below the canopies of the trees, the Cloud following just behind them got caught in the branches, and disintegrated into shards of glass which fell in tiny pieces onto the ground. The soil on that December night was very moist and the pieces of glass were absorbed quickly.

Pauline continued towards the lake with the sixty petits yiyis flying only a few inches above the cold water. The clouds which had managed to avoid bumping into the branches of the tall trees were closing in on them. Pauline remembered her first vision, when she had seen the Rainlights diving into the sea, at the Beginning of Humanity. She slowed down and just as the clouds were about to catch up with them she dived into the cold water, followed by the other five Vs. The Clouds tried to follow them and crashed into the water, this time the shards of glass hit the water, bounced against the surface of the lake and then back up, smashing into the Clouds which had stayed above. Pauline was simply following the teaching of Zhi Ruo, using the opponent's strength to his detriment.

Pauline's petits yiyis resurfaced after a few hundred metres. The clouds had been beaten- all but one- perhaps the leader?

She flew out of the woods and back towards Paris, this time to the South Circular, and accelerated. The Cloud was not as fast, which explained how the children had managed to hide the Refugees in the Jardin des Plantes without being noticed.

At the Porte d'Italie, one of the exits of the South Circular, she veered left, and followed the motorway. There was a signpost reading Marché International de Rungis, the largest food market in Europe, with gigantic cold rooms, huge refrigerated trucks and cabinets. The petits yiyis were at the international market within minutes. Fresh food arrived here daily from all over Europe, so it was open 24/7, with most of the business conducted during the night.

Pauline gave instructions to her five friends.

They split up, hovering above the market, waiting for the last cloud.

Each group petits yiyis was now looking for an empty refrigerated truck.

The Cloud released a part of itself every time it saw a V-shaped squadron and that part tried to catch it.

Nafissatou's team was the first to play hide and seek. She flew inside a refrigerated truck at full speed, stopped short at the end, summersaulted towards the ceiling, and accelerated back out of the truck, the part of the Cloud following her crashed inside. She focused hard on the door, which closed, and lowered the handle, laughing to herself she thought of the person who would open it in another country in a few hours.

Pauline, Fatima, Sarah, Zhi Ruo and Aurelio repeated the same game all over the market. They managed to close the truck doors behind them and trap the Angries and their stench. It was not fair on the transporters, who would have to give their trucks a serious clean, but anything goes in love and war.

Chapter Twelve

Finally, the Christmas holidays arrived, two whole weeks. Pauline's father would stay behind, in Paris, since the festivities would draw an even larger number of tourists to the capital who would celebrate into the early hours of the night on Christmas Eve and even more on New Year's Eve

This was the first festive period she was going to spend without her father, and sadly, the second without her mother.

He took her by train, which was much quicker and avoided the traffic jams in the North of Paris, to Roissy Charles-de-Gaulle Airport. Pauline was in two minds about the trip, on the one hand, she was going to miss the presence of her father, and it would never be same, now that her mother was gone, but on the other hand, she would spend two weeks with Giorgos, a cousin of her father's- who she called Uncle Yorgi. He was the same age as her father, but blonde and blue-eyed, quite unusual colouring for a Greek man, but Zakynthos, the island where he lived, had been occupied by the Venetians for four centuries and even his name was of Italian origin.

It was the first time that Pauline had flown on her own, at the check-in, a hostess, specially designated to look after children travelling without an adult, had placed a big board around her neck- which made her look like a walking parcel -so that she could be shown to her place in the plane, and then checked on periodically all along the journey.

Her plane left at 12, and three hours later, she would arrive in Athens, walk a few metres to a gate and wait for a second flight, nicknamed the hopper by the locals. She wondered what the petits yiyis would make of that trip in the air, without flying themselves.

A total of 6 hours later, she landed on the island of Zakynthos and was greeted by her Uncle Yorgi. He was a little taller than her father, but the same build, he was also very discreet about his past. She wondered whether they had not been brothers in arms and when she watched 24 or Homeland on TV, she wondered if perhaps they had had similar experiences.

Uncle Yorgi did not speak a word of French, but a little German and very good English. Pauline endeavoured to use the few words of Greek she had learnt over many holidays but needed to brush up on every time she returned.

Without knowing why, she had always been attracted to the island, on the West side of the mainland and she remembered her vision of the Beginning of Humanity with the olive trees, the Rainlights and the Angries.

Uncle Yorgi was always smiling. He lived in the low mountains, with Auntie Siobhan and their three children. The journey by car from the airport to Katastari took half an hour and by the time they arrived at his stone house she knew everything that had taken place on the island since last summer.

After the meal, they all sat outside, by the yellow and blue flames of logs burning in a barrel. The temperature was nothing like Paris, no snow and no harsh wind, but not warm enough to wear just a T-shirt. Uncle Yorgi, with eyes lit up like a child's, was describing the stars, the constellations. Was he a Rainlight? She wondered.

She could not believe that all children inevitably became Angries. On the other hand, when she thought of the bullies in her school, they were closer to being Angries than to Rainlights.

She did not know how to bring the conversation round to her experiences of the last few weeks. She wanted to be cautious. Uncle Yorgi was a dreamer and would probably not laugh at her, but if he was worried, he would surely talk to her father and he, in turn, might be upset that she had hidden her big secret from him.

She had an idea: "Are there any legends about the origin of the olive trees, and how they appeared on the island?" she asked innocently.

Uncle Yorgi looked at her, amazed. Why would she want to know that?

Pauline wondered whether he knew, or if he could feel that she was concerned about them and why?

He began to smile, but quickly put on a more serious face.

"Nobody knows exactly. Some say the first tree came from Israel, at the time of King Solomon, around 960 BC, when an envoy from the King planted the first olive tree on the island, as a token of friendship with the inhabitants".

Something for me to ask Sarah, Pauline thought, she came from Israel so she could get more information from her family.

"Another legend says that Mary Magdalene came to the island in 34 AD, one year after Jesus died on the cross, and planted the first olive tree in the North, between Kabi and Volimes and that tree is still there. Every year, before the harvest, in November, the villagers gather round it and pray for a successful yield. Indeed, olive trees are essential for us. We use everything from the tree: the fruit to make oil, the branches and twigs for fireplaces and the trunks to make wooden boards for houses."

Pauline was trying to remember all that.

"We have more than two million trees on the island, most of them are hundreds of years old."

So far, what he was saying tied up with what she already knew, but she did not pluck up the courage to mention the petits yiyis, Rainlights, Angries, or the Refugees.

Everything felt so peaceful on the island, so different from Paris. She fell asleep, hoping her petits yiyis would not decide to visit Zakynthos by night.

When she woke up the following morning, she was elated to see that they had stayed connected to her feet, since there was no trace of earth or of olive twigs on them. Perhaps there were NO Refugees on the island because there was NO danger here for them.

She could imagine planes from all around the world bringing Refugees to the island. Actually, she wondered whether it was the same on other islands. She remembered the first time she had googled the olive tree and seen that there were hundreds of islands situated on the Mediterranean Sea, so perhaps they could provide a safe haven for all the older and abandoned petits yiyis scattered all over the world.

She knew that there is a one hour time difference between France and Greece, so she waited a bit before Facetiming Sarah. She emailed her to gather the other five together and they arranged to communicate later that morning.

"The connection may break up any time," Pauline said after they had all exchanged greetings. She told her friends about the olive trees on the island, knowing that they would each try to gather more information. Also she asked whether any more toxic clouds had appeared.

"It's amazing how easy it was to dispose of them," Nafissatou said. "When you think they contained shards of glass that could have damaged our petits yiyis!" she added.

"I wonder whether they are not victims of their own anger" Zhi Ruo commented. "Did you notice that the more they chased us, the easier it became to defeat them?"

"Indeed," Fatima joined in, "they seemed to be blind with hatred. They got caught in the branches of the trees of the Bois de Vincennes, then crashed onto the cold water of the lake and finally, left themselves locked inside refrigerated trucks. You can't say that they are very bright!"

They all paused, reflecting on what it could mean, for the future.

"What about you?" Aurelio asked.

Pauline raised the webcam from Uncle Yorgi's screen and turned it towards the window. They could see that there was no snow, but a clear blue sky and many branches laden with fruit on the olive trees.

"The olive harvest started last month and will continue to the end of February," Pauline said , proud to show that she had learnt a bit from Uncle Yorgi, then thousands of litres of olive oil will be sent from the island to many places in the world.

The other five children also set their grey cells in motion, like pinions rotating faster and faster in a timepiece mechanism. Then another light bulb moment, "Is this the link we have been looking for?" Sarah ventured. "We wondered why some Rainlights, became Angries and others did not."

"Yes," Nafissatou continued, "we know it started a long, long time before our computer networks, and smart phones and could not understand how the Angries communicated, and spread, like viruses."

"Think of it, every tree can bear 30 to 50 kilos olives, and it takes about 5 kilos to make a litre of oil." Pauline stated.

"And you say that on Zakynthos alone, there are 2 million trees. So how many millions of trees exist from Portugal to the Middle-East, then down and back to Morocco?" Sarah was trying to work out aloud.

"You would only need to poison a few fields here and there, and the disease would spread like the flu" Fatima said, frightened.

"But where does the poison come from?" Aurelio asked.

"Remember the Clouds disintegrating and turning into stinking shards of glass, containing hate-filled faces? Perhaps evil thoughts, when they are put into action, leave traces- like the fumes from the exhaust pipe of a car- then collect into little fogs that increase in size and become Clouds."

"Right, you mean that these Clouds are the garbage collectors of evil human actions, and that once above the olive groves, they disintegrate, and plant their shards into the soil to poison the trees, like injecting a virus in a vein?" Nafissatou remarked.

"So the villagers harvest the fruit, thinking they are producing good oil, but they are in fact sending infected oil to millions of people, turning them into Angries- the cycle is never-ending."Zhi Ruo replied, her eyes wide open in disgust.

"Perhaps some people resist better than others, and keep their milk petits yiyis and remain Rainlights, while others prefer to give in to hatred, and jealousy, happy to inflict pain and see other people suffer, then their milk petits yiyis are abandoned leaving room for wisdom/hate-filled petits yiyis"? Aurelio thought aloud.

They stared at each other.

"How can we stop them, or will we be able we stop them at all?" asked Fatima

"We have been chosen," Pauline replied, "there must be a reason!"

She did not know which one and this was exactly the moment when the Internet connection broke up.

Chapter Thirteen

Pauline was beginning to see more clearly, the task was at least twofold, but for the time being, she wanted to keep things plain and simple. She and her five friends needed to bring as many Refugees as they could to safety, and curb the spread of the Angries.

Which was more urgent, to discover where the Refugees were hiding, all over the world and try to rescue as many as possible before they disappeared, or to find out which oils were contaminated and try to prevent them from reaching the tables of innocent Rainlights?

She had asked her friends to do some research into the sale of olive oil in their respective countries of origin, where they had relatives, and to see if they could find similar legends to those Uncle Yorgi told her about the arrival of the olive tree on his island of Zakynthos. Surely, there must be tales like that in China, Africa, South America, and the Ancient Middle-East!

Now she was in Uncle Yorgi's car. His three children were aged between 15 and 21 and did not really care for baby-sitting young Pauline, even less during the 'Yortes Christouyennon' (Christmas holidays).

Uncle Yorgi was running around all the time and she enjoyed discovering the life of a working adult. She had spent some time listening to her father singing in the restaurants near the Moulin-Rouge, but it wasn't real work, but more of a pleasure, and the tips from the

Japanese, Asians and Americans were often very good.

Uncle Yorgi spent his life going from one administration office to another, presenting papers, being told that another one was needed, and then a civil servant would proudly put a stamp on the mysterious paper and enable him to go to another office, wait, present another paper, and so on and so forth. It was a sheer waste of time, but he said that everything had to be done by the letter, to be legit, because selling land and building a house were no easy matters.

"It's a little like a treasure hunt!" Pauline exclaimed, as they parked on Alexandrou Roma, the main street of Zante, the Capital in the South of the island, with its curved harbour and two ferry ports.

He laughed, "yes, absolutely!"

After a morning spent obtaining permits and ordering materials from big stores- always with the presentation of papers and people putting stamps on them- they stopped for a snack, it was eleven o'clock so they had café frappes- cold coffees- with huge croissants.

"Bravo, orea! (very well, perfect)" Uncle Yorgi said, always happy to make at least some progress on his quest to complete a house.

"Would you like to see the real work I do?" he asked.

"Yes, please Uncle Yorgi!"

They took the road towards the airport, did not turn left but carried on towards Lithakia.

After following a long, winding road, he pulled up by a beach, not unusual since the island had more than one hundred beaches!

"This is Turtle Island," he pointed. Indeed, the rock emerging from the sea looked like a turtle on the sand protecting her eggs, the head pointing to the South and a big hump behind, like the body. "This is where they lay thousands of eggs every year," he said, on this 'liyi yi'.

Pauline flinched. What did her petits yiyis have to do with this, her father used to call her toes that ever since she could remember, but Uncle Yorgi?

"What did you say, Uncle Yorgi?" she asked, a little gob smacked.

"I meant a little plot of land, liyi yi- in Greek 'liyi' means a little and 'yi' means plot of land," he replied, hesitantly, as if he had put his foot in it, Pauline thought, but in what? Was it pure coincidence that her father had nicknamed her toes 'petit yiyis'? Especially now she knew that they were not standard toes, but toes that could fly away and return home, like remote controlled drones that enabled her friends and herself to discover a world of mysteries, a world of danger as well.

She could see olive trees on Turtle Island, just opposite the small village of Agios Sostis. She decided to push her luck a bit. "What does Agios Sostis mean?"

Uncle Yorgi looked at her, just like her father did when she was asking a tricky question, as if gauging the extent of what he should say to help on her quest for knowledge, without downloading too much information into her head in one go.

Agios means holy and Sostis correct, as a teacher says 'sosta' when you give the right answer to a question"

He showed her a few properties he had built in the area over the years. He said he always endeavoured to move as few trees as he could. "The older they are the harder they are to transplant and success is never certain, because some of the roots are very long, and interwoven, and the trunks can split, as if struck by lightning."

Pauline could already picture herself repeating all this to her friends next time they Facetimed.

At that time of the year, many places on the island looked like a deserted country after a war, or a bombing. Hotels and restaurants were closed from November to late April on most parts of the island.

"This would be a good time to bring the Refugees here, as there is almost nobody to spy on us if we did" she thought to herself. But every solution posed its own problem- she had to go back to school at the beginning of January and would probably not be back to Zakynthos before the summer as her father might send her to her mother's parents in Arhus, Denmark, for Easter.

So far, the children could control the flight of their petits yiyis for a few kilometres, but from Paris to Zakynthos, you're talking 2500 km! No way can we fly, let alone tow and drag hundreds of tired Refugees over such a distance! She thought for a minute of migratory birds and had an idea, a long shot, but an idea all the same.

***

Evenings in Greece are often a time for celebration and, unlike in Paris, children are taken to the restaurants with the adults and can stay late, not so much because the adults want to get them used to celebrating, but because baby-sitters are expensive and this way parents can keep an eye on their progeny.

This evening, Uncle Yorgi had organised dinner, with dancing, in the mountains, with some of his co-workers

The drill is always the same, people start eating and drinking at around 9/10 o'clock, at a time when most Parisians have usually finished dining. The musicians start playing at 9, not too loudly, and then, as the tables are cleared, conversations become more animated, and they start group dances, very much like traditional line dances in the South of the USA. Everybody joins in, young and old, rich and poor, it does not matter.

Pauline was waiting for The Zeibekiko. The first time she saw it, she had been a toddler and she had cried. It was devised by adults for adults, or to be more specific, by warriors, 3 centuries ago. They would form a circle round a bonfire, clap their hands in the rhythm of a slow flamenco, while one of them moved into the centre, and according to their physical ability, would walk forward, rotate, walk back, sway, kneel, or jump, the most expert would even balance a glass on their foreheads, or shoulders.

Uncle Yorgi explained, (and she never spoilt his joy at describing the ways of his ancestors, letting him tell the same story for the umpteenth time) that it was originally, a holy dance, to ward off evil spirits, take away pain and ask others for their support. Those around the edge of the circle would clap their hands for the one in the middle, regardless of whether he or she, was a friend or a complete stranger.

The musicians started to play THE ZEIBEKIKO, and Uncle Yorgi stood up, followed by half a dozen mates.

About twenty diners formed a circle made up of friends and strangers alike. Someone started to dance the basic steps in the middle. It was the tradition that amateur dancers went first, then young people, sometimes even children, then more expert dancers, then finally, a complete beginner, for his initiation- as if to tell him or her, he or she was accepted as part of the Greek Community. The candidate never knew in advance, it was always a surprise. He or she would be brought to the circle, usually on one knee, clapping their hands, and then, the one in the centre would stop dancing, walk towards the candidate, and pull him or her into the centre, to take his place. This was deemed an honour and no one was expected to cry off. Every Greek in his life experienced the nervousness of this first time, the shyness, and embarrassment, it was part of the culture. Uncle Yorgi was an accomplished dancer, throwing his legs up, bending backwards, and then doing a kind of push-up to pick up a glass on the floor. Pauline was clapping her hands on one knee, as Uncle Yorgi had shown her and she was doing it with complete dedication.

She had seen her father doing this dance, many times. He had said that it was Uncle Yorgi who had pulled him into the circle for the first time, when they were teenagers. Her father, in turn, had pulled her mother into the circle, probably the first German/Danish lady to be admitted to the dance that symbolised the union of the soul and the body, dreams and expectations with reality. She always wondered whether her day would come to dance, like a few children she had seen.

She clapped her hands, moved by the music, a sad song, about impossible love, a man realising that the lady he loved would never reciprocate, like the ones that she had heard her father sing in Paris.

As she looked at Uncle Yorgi dancing, she thought that he must have kept his milk petits yiyis and in spite of his one metre eighty-five and muscles, was still a Rainlight, like many people on the island.

She could see tears rolling down his cheeks, focused on the music he was dancing to. She looked round, and saw that some members of the circle also seemed moved by his dancing.

Suddenly he stopped and looked at her. Pauline was petrified. He advanced towards her, held out his hand and, to the cheers of an encouraging crowd, pulled her gently into the circle, to take his place, knelt down and start to clap his hands, looking at her with reassuring eyes.

Chapter Fourteen

« To ekana kai i kori sou chorepse poli kala (I did and your daughter danced very well) » Pauline overheard Uncle Yorgi say on the telephone the following morning.

So Uncle Yorgi had told her father!

It had been a big day and a lot to take in, the Greek meaning of petits yiyis, Turtle Island and its olive trees, opposite a place called Holy Right -away from the rest of the world, on a little plot of land – many coincidences!

And the icing on the cake, her first Greek holy dance. She would never forget that night, dancing her first Zeibekiko. Now she was formally and publicly accepted as a member of the community. "I'd better improve my Greek if I want to take part in the life of the island," she thought. Luckily, Greek and German are similar, the words are constructed in the same way and the pronunciation not too complicated.

Pauline had started the day with her Tai-Chi exercise outside on the stone patio, in December, something she could never do in Paris unless she wanted to catch pneumonia.

It was Sunday and Yorgi wouldn't go to work, at least he wouldn't go to see any civil servants, but, much to Siobhan's sadness, he might check on a couple of building sites in the morning, because the rule was simple, no work no pay he explained to Pauline.

In Greece, Sunday lunch is taken rather late, at 2 if not 3 o'clock, after a little snack around 11 and of course breakfast at dawn, for those who had an early night. A light breakfast, consisted of Greek yoghurt and honey, thanks to the millions of bees living on the island.

So there she was on a deck chair, with just a blanket over her legs and body. The view from Katastari was stunning, she could see the Salt Flats of Alykes just at her feet, Alykanas to her right, then the hills leading to Tsilivi, and across the sea, the continent.

On her left, the taller island of Kefalonia could be seen, the tops of its mountains covered in snow **for** several weeks of the year.

She had an idea: Auntie Siobhan was cleaning the house, washing the clothes, etc. inside, and the three adolescents, Ruby, Joe and Mat, were either asleep, or pounding on their tablets and i-pads in their rooms.

There was nobody in sight. She removed her shoes, and her socks, then put the blanket back on, with a little open space underneath.

She started to concentrate, feeling the cicadas slowly vibrating, then the petits yiyis left her feet, found their way underneath the blanket and assumed the V-shaped reconnaissance formation. They were floating in the air, a couple of feet in front of Pauline. She glanced around quickly, lest any of the three siblings or Auntie Siobhan could see her. No, there was nothing but absolute quietness. She guided her petits yiyis towards the road below, turned right towards the main road of Katastari, turned left at the hairpin junction, at the top of the road and then straight on for about 16 km, easy to follow in the daylight, but she would not have tried it in the middle of the night, because, unlike in Paris, she could not resort to a Plan B, like the Bateaux-Mouches or buses. Arriving at the crossroads leading to the city centre, ahead or the airport to the right, she turned right. Her squadron was flying fast, probably 120 km/h, so nobody would have time to notice them, also they were a hundred feet above ground, with no fear of colliding with a sky-scraper as there were none on the island!

She decided to turn left towards the airport, then turned left again towards Kalamaki, a long, long road, filled with restaurants, bursting to capacity in the warmer months, a ghost town in the cooler months. Now she was close to the sea and simply hovered above it gently. She turned right and followed the beach, leaving the dunes and woods on her right, a marvellous place to walk she thought and to hide as well. She flew over Laganas Beach, then arrived at Agios Sostis, with the village of Lithakia further up. She hesitated a bit, would it disturb the turtles if her petits yiyis landed on their island? How big, was their island anyway, she wondered, perhaps the size of a football pitch or a little bigger?

She landed on the tip of the head of the turtle-shaped rock and waited. She could see a few turtles, some probably three foot long and weighing 100 kilos, swimming leisurely with no sign of panic. These must be on guard duty. Uncle Yorgi had told her that the mating season, when thousands of eggs were laid, was between April and June, with the baby turtles hatching six to eight weeks after the eggs have been hidden in the sand. A mother turtle laid more than 100 eggs at a time every two weeks, if she reckoned correctly, that was 600 eggs per female. She could not see any very old olive trees on the two rocks emerging from the sea that formed Turtle Island. The older trees, have the most intricate roots and trunks, like faces, and snakes curled up around columns, and branches coming down and up again, appearing to express all sorts of emotions.

On the island there were only a few olive trees, but not tall, these were young trees as you see in a nursery. Would the olives from these trees fall where the turtles hatched, stick to the unsuspecting young turtles, like hitchhiker's rucksacks, and then become scattered all over the world, wherever the turtles travelled? Would they meet other petits yiyis and become Rainlights, like at the beginning of humanity? Were the young turtles unsuspecting, or - the thought made Pauline laugh - perhaps they acted as a kind of Internet, transmitting messages? It seemed more plausible.

Apparently the Rainlights born from olives were few and far between and almost all of them came from humans, with a portion of Rainlights being passed on from generation to generation, with mixed fortunes.

Uncle Yorgi had told her that turtles could vocalise, and produce very low frequency calls of short duration. Like an alarm, a fire alarm in a supermarket, she thought. But mostly, they communicated through vibrations.

Perhaps the turtles were protecting the pure olive trees all around the island, and giving news and the latest gossip about life on the island to the Refugees all over the world, providing they were close to a beach.

She saw another possibility: the island is isolated, and by law, people are banned from going there, or sailing too close and causing pollution from their engines, so, instead of a nursery, it could it be a hospital for convalescent Refugees, or even forsaken petits yiyis who could finish their existence there. The island would act like a reservoir, a library of memories that the young turtles would then use to fuel the never-ending cycle of Hope against Anger?

"So you're ready to take over?" she heard a voice behind her and instantly froze with fear. It was Ruby, the daughter of Yorgi and Siobhan. Like Pauline, she was a mixture of several nationalities and languages-Irish and English through her mother, Greek and Italian through her father- like her she was pale-skinned, blue-eyed, with long, light-coloured hair, and already tall, not far from one metre eighty at only 15.

Pauline did not know what to say. She prayed that Ruby would not lift the blanket to see the empty mooring stations at the end of her feet.

Ruby walked round the deckchair, matter-of-factly, under the pleading eyes of Pauline. She lifted the blanket briefly, then let it drop back in place.

"Don't worry," she said. "I've done my share when I was your age, and a little more as you will see it's only the beginning "leaving Pauline with even more questions than at the start of her "trip" to the Turtle Island.

She waited for Ruby to go back to the house, brought her reconnaissance squadron, this time following the beach to Zante, above the two ferry ports, then over the hills of Bokhali, over the beach of Tsilivi and hugging the shore back to Alykes and finally resuming their normal stations.

She remained motionless for a while, not daring to go to the house in case Ruby had said anything to her brothers, whose gaze Pauline did not want to cross right now.

A van pulled up by the heavy metal gate, always closed to prevent the dog from escaping.

Auntie Siobhan came out and opened the gate for the driver to enter carrying two huge cold boxes, followed by Auntie Siobhan with a couple of shopping bags.

"This is Jas," she said to Pauline, who was happy to be able to stand up now that she had put her socks and shoes back on. "He often commutes between Zakynthos and Europe." And before Pauline had the time to ask anything, she heard the man say, in a very low-pitched voice. "Yes, I bring stray dogs for adoption to the North of Europe and on the way back, as my truck is empty, I bring food and alcohol to the expats on the island, or to those who like French and Italian food and wines."

"So you drive all the way from Paris?" the little girl asked, with a new idea in mind.

"Yes, and I take the ferry from Ancona to Patras, it takes 24 hours and I can relax. Then, one hour and a half to Killini, on the continent, and finally, the ferry, to Zante town."

The little girl thought, "if he could transport thousands of Refugees he could solve a big problem.

"He is not just a transporter, he also impersonates Elvis Presley in restaurants on the island in the summer!" Siobhan added joyfully and he started to sing "Love me tender, love me sweet "He had something in common with her father.

"By the way, before I forget" Jas said, extracting a parcel from one of the shopping bags Siobhan had carried, "this is from your father, for Christmas."

She took it, amazed that father knew this man.

"Come on, open it!" he added with his heavyweight boxing champion voice.

It was a tablet. "I shan't need to borrow Uncle Yorgi's computer any more" she thought.

She stood on tiptoe to reach his unshaven cheeks and kissed him as she would a member of the family.

"Give my regards to your father!" he said when he about to leave. "Strange," Pauline thought, "he has the same build as Uncle Yorgi and my father. Did they all meet when they were young, in some kind of secret organisation? There was something funny in the way Uncle Yorgi, Ruby and now this man, Jas, turned up with answers to questions Pauline had on her mind.

Chapter Fifteen

"You see Pauline, the Internet is not always reliable on this part of the island," Ruby said, pointing to the beaches of Alykes, where Pauline said she would like to go for a Facetime meeting with her friends, who had remained in cold and snowy Paris.

Ruby had skilfully avoided Pauline's company since she had let on that she was glad the French girl was taking over. But taking over what? Pauline would have liked to ask. She felt as if her progress had to be slow and gradual, as if she needed time to understand what was going on, and make her own decisions. She felt that someone was guiding her on a sort of treasure hunt, leaving clues here and there for her to follow. Every time she thought she was getting to the bottom of it, that she was finding a solution, a greater problem loomed. But it was exciting and, she was not alone, she had Nafissatou, Fatima, Sarah, Zhi Ruo and Aurelio, each with their suggestions.

She took her tablet in a bag and walked down the steep road towards the Salt Flats, minding her steps, so as not to fall and break her brand new tablet. Uncle Yorgi had put a 4G key in so she should be able to get a decent connection. He always saw the better side of life, even if she could see sadness in his eyes at times.

She walked past the Hotel Maria on her right. She realised that it was the first time in her life that she had been allowed to wander alone, without adults or other children. Although, when she turned around she saw

Ruby on the patio outside her parents' house, a hundred feet above her, keeping watch.

She continued straight on, and reached the Salt Flats, filled up to the rim, as an artificial retention basin for the heavy rainfalls between November and April and used to water the plants of the island during the warmer months, when no rain fell, so that there were no desert areas. The island absorbed the rain like a sponge, then released it slowly, like a drip to a patient in hospital- although unlike a hospital patient the vegetation looked extremely healthy.

A couple of minutes later, she was on one of the beaches, Alykes, and took her tablet out. It was late morning and she had sent messages to her friends so they would be ready and waiting for her in Sarah's flat.

"Good morning, my friends," she said, seeing their faces 2,500 km away, clustered around the screen. "Kalimera!" the five of them exclaimed joyfully, happy to show that they knew how to greet a person in Greek.

She recounted her Initiation into the traditional dance, her trip to Turtle Island and Jas, the transporter, whom she suggested they could try and use to bring as many Refugees as possible from France, to the place of safety that she saw off the shore of Agios Sostis.

"It's funny that your father called your toes petit yiyis, now that you have told us that "liyi yi" means 'a small plot of land," Sarah said.

"Do you think it's a pure coincidence?" Nafissatou asked.

"You mentioned that this guy, Jas, and Uncle Yorgi, if you don't mind my calling him that , are friends, and that they have known each other for many years". Zhi

Ruo stated. "You even suspect that they might have been part of a secret organisation."

"Perhaps they did the same as us, when they were young?" Aurelio ventured.

The thought of the three middle-aged men flying their toes above the cities made Pauline giggle, and as if her friends shared her vision, they also laughed.

"But Ruby, Uncle Yorgi's and Auntie Siobhan's daughter," Fatima intervened, "can we ask her for help? She told you it was only the beginning."

"The beginning of what?" Nafissatou wanted to know.

"It seems that we are being led to discover what we have to do little by little, so as not to fail or to lose fath." Pauline replied. "Look, so far, we have rescued hundreds of Refugees and defeated clouds of Angries twice."

"Yes, but there may be millions of abandoned milk petits yiyis all around the world, waiting to be rescued before they disintegrate, and take with them, pieces of Hope. How do we find them?" Fatima asked.

"Perhaps they leave clues when they are abandoned" Aurelio said.

"But how? They can't write, they can't make signposts, there must be something else, which is obvious but that we can't see" Sarah continued.

They all remained silent for a while.

"Ruby said that it was only the beginning" Zhi Ruo stated, thinking hard. "Perhaps there are places dedicated to Refugees, that Rescuers of all times and all countries, children like us, have indicated, for the next generation of Rescuers to find to resume the salvation process where the previous team had stopped."

"I like your idea, very much!" Pauline commented.

"Perhaps we are part of a long, never-ending team of Rescuers ..." Aurelio, said, dreaming aloud, "like Gladiators, Knight Templars, Musketeers, and Navy Seals. Well sort of!"

"If that is so, our predecessors have left clues in their own language all over the world."

"Hang on a minute," Nafissatou broke in, "countries have been invaded, dismantled and merged with others, and thousands of languages have disappeared."

There was another pause.

"But some languages have been preserved for many centuries, like Hebrew, Chinese, Arabic, Hieroglyphics" Fatima stated.

"And Greek" Pauline said.

"Unless some Rescuers made a mixture of languages, a secret one, a kind of code which could be understood regardless of whether you speak German, Italian, Hebrew, Arabic, Russian, Greek, etc." Sarah said, "because they could not know what the future would hold in their countries, so they had to choose a multi-user tool."

"What about Africa and South America?" Nafissatou asked, "Writing is very new, although the Mayas, the Aztecs and the Incas left signs on their temples. Think of the thousands of tribes living in the mountains and in the forests that tell stories which pass, from generation to generation, when even the dialects change a little from one valley to the next."

Once again, the six children were silent.

"Perhaps the situation is not so critical in places on the planet which are still undamaged" Aurelio said. "Where Nature can look after Herself without Rescuers, or where the tribes have looked after their environment from generation to generation and the Angries are not a danger."

"Yes," Fatima continued, "it would make sense. Writing was invented to communicate, for people to preserve the traditions of the past and present, feeling that the future may not be so bright"

"And some of them-the Rescuers- used signs, letters, figures, words sounds and symbols that the Angries could not decipher" Zhi Ruo thought aloud.

"Providing a Rescuer did not betray the team and give the code to the Angries,' Pauline said.

"Hang on" Fatima asked. "If we agree that there have been Rescuers since the dawn of Humanity, and that each generation takes over from the previous one to save the Refugees, then there must be the same on the other side, the dark side, perhaps Demolishers, Busters, Destroyers, I don't know what to call them. If we are needed to save the Refugees, then obviously, there must be teams, chasing the Refugees, from generation to generation."

They all looked to the skies for inspiration, trying to imagine who the Destroyers were. The clouds of shards of glass with angry faces, where did they live, how did they communicate? Did they shadow the Rescuers, were they former Rescuers turned to the Evil side? Like an employee of a big company who sells industrial secrets to another to make more money and gain power, or a soldier who betrays his brothers-in-arms and defects to the other side? They all seem to follow the same trains of thought since, at the end, they all gave a sigh, as if theirs brains were filled with question marks.

At that moment, Pauline saw bubbles growing from strength to strength at the surface of the sea, some thirty metres from the shore where she was standing. She turned her tablet around from her friends so that they could all see what was happening.

"What a wonderful view you have!" Sarah exclaimed, at first.

"What's that?" Aurelio asked, as the bubbles turned into spheres floating above the water. Gradually, translucent spheres piled up in three columns, four in the centre, the lowest one touching the gentle waves, and then the left and right column rose a bit, and they contained three spheres each.

"That's me," Zhi Ruo screamed.

Indeed, the face of the little girl appeared in the sphere which was barely touching the water, and then they could see the face disappear from one sphere and form in another, climbing from one sphere to the next, in a zig-zag pattern. Each sphere had its own coloured background, figures, letters, words, and symbols were flashing each time the face appeared in one of them.

The children were frightened at first.

"Look!" Zhi Ruo said, calmer now, "this is me, growing up, I am smiling, in the second sphere in the middle column, then in the first column on the right, I seem to be thinking hard, with a finger on my lips and then, oooo, I am in the first sphere on the left, talking to an invisible crowd and I look a little older."

Her image continued its zig-zag progression, with her features growing older, sometimes looking joyful in the spheres of the right column, and stern, serious, in the spheres of the left column, and becoming simply calm in those in the centre, each time with signs flashing and against a different colour background…

The top sphere, in the centre, above the top left and the top right, showed a colour and signs, but no face.

Then each began the same process: Nafissatou, Fatima, Sarah, Aurelio and, to finish Pauline, except that for each child, the signs were not always the same, as if customised.

"This is us growing up" said Pauline. "The Spheres are like Facebook posts from the future, of course in the past, there was no such thing, so this could be what the Rescuers used, these Spheres. I don't know how they do it, but perhaps we can see our futures, with variations."

"Yes," Sarah observed, the images were flashing faster and there were more and more, in rapid succession in a Sphere, as they were climbing. "This is strange."

"It was as if we saw what could be, good and bad, and what we could do for others or just for ourselves, with kindness or with selfishness," Fatima added.

"Did you see that?" Nafissatou said, after a moment. "The petits yiyis were flashing at the bottom of the spheres, like warning lights. Sometimes we looked like Rainlights, and at others like Angries. We saw it in the Spheres!"

"You know, perhaps it was staring at us all along ..."
Pauline ventured. "Perhaps we are part of the code"

Chapter Sixteen

Only one more day on the island with Uncle Yorgi, Auntie Siobhan, Ruby and her two brothers and then the holiday would be over. Pauline had spoken to her mother a few times and told her about what she had found. Her mother had listened to her, visibly happy to see that her daughter was making progress in her quest. Pauline would have liked her to come back, to live with them, physically, not just inside her green whirl pool. It was as if two worlds were at the interface of each other, touching each other, existing in parallel but sometimes, with gateways, like linking two computers of a different make with an adapter. The green whirl pool was the adapter. "Actually it's a bit like the Spheres which had formed above the sea, at Alykes beach" Pauline said to herself. "Not real as we understand it, but still, real enough to leave memories and feelings."

As usual, she was doing her morning Tai-Chi exercises in Uncle Yorgi's olive grove. She loved every minute of it, sheltered from the rest of the world, and in tune with timeless Nature. A slight wind rustled the branches. She imagined the olives falling, turning into petits yiyis, giving birth to Rainlights who had spread life and love at the beginning of humanity, and now gave fruit, oil, wood for furniture and building, wood for use in fireplaces, and what else?

She remembered the clouds of shards of glass filled with angry faces chasing the children's petits yiyis in the Bois de Vincennes, and how the branches acted as shields, letting the Rescuers through unscathed and disintegrating the Clouds pursuing them.

Perhaps the trees in the world had other, even better purposes.

She was bending her body gently, breathing in and out deeply. She had the impression she could hear the vibrations of the leaves falling onto the ground, the insects collecting food and the vibrations of the trees. There was no apparition, no vision, just the feeling of being a chord of a harp, stroked by the air waves surrounding her.

The more she thought gently and respectfully of the trees, the insects, the leaves, the rocks, the more pleasant feelings she was experienced. It was like an invisible dialogue between fixed elements, with her, moving among them, as if she had taken a book from a shelf and enjoyed reading it. These trees and the nature around, below and above them felt like pages to read, voices to be heard, feelings to be shared. Her mind was floating from one story to another. She looked at a very old tree, probably 800 years old, judging by the width of the trunk, six feet in diameter, split in the middle with each side bending away from the centre. Unlike Pauline doing her exercises, the two parts would never unite, stayed in the same position and had taken centuries to bend, instead of the couple of seconds it took her. "There I am, tiny and mobile, and there they are timeless and fixed, evolving very, very slowly." she said to herself, smiling.

Perhaps trees are the guardians of our thoughts, like recorders or registrars. We produce images in our minds and instead of vanishing in the air, they are caught by the branches, and stored there as in the hard drive of a desktop. The trees observe, note down, and place pictures of our thoughts, feelings and actions in tiny compartments in their leaves, ready to be browsed by humble and sincere seekers. This way, perhaps, everything we experience, joy and sadness, all our memories, never die but are simply uploaded into the trees for eternity.

She needed her friends to know all this and decided to put it all down on her tablet once she completed her meditation. She wouldn't be surprised her friends were sharing the same feelings, perhaps she could contact them across the 2500 km between Zakynthos and Paris. Perhaps Zhi Ruo had also unlocked a door in her mind, with her meditation practice.

***

Now the moment she dreaded most was coming, her last evening in Zakynthos. In a way she was happy to see her father, her friends and the Refugees that they had left in the Jardin des Plantes. She was especially keen to look for those that they did not have a clue as to their whereabouts. But life on the Greek island felt secure, with the trees, the turtles in Agios Sostis, slower and not so cold. Oh, she was not that naïve, there must be some Angries among the population, like everywhere else, but there, they seem less dangerous, as far as she could tell.

Uncle Yorgi and Auntie Siobhan had invited twenty friends or so, to celebrate the New Year, in a huge tavern, called Popolaros, near Lithakia, not far from Turtle Island. There was live music and after ten o'clock the diners started to dance off the gorgeous meals they had enjoyed.

115

One of the dances was the Hasapiko. The first letter had to be pronounced as the CH in Lochness or in German "Ach". Auntie Siobhan was leading the line, and eight people joined her as Uncle Yorgi took the microphone. He started to sing "Matia Vourkomenia" (misty eyes, i.e. filled with tears), a song about the sadness of those who had to leave their native land, hoping to find a brighter future somewhere else. She remembered her father singing Country and Western songs from Alabama or Tennessee with a similar message. Yes, sadness could be found all over the planet.

Pauline was letting her mind wander round the room and gradually could see thoughts rising from the diners, as she had on a bus a few weeks before in Paris. Some people sitting at the tables were smiling and talking to each other, but the faces displayed above theirs head showed completely different attitudes, some were far, far away, picturing images of their offices, homes, or holidays, sometimes against a background of joyful colours like yellow or orange, others looking at people across the table or sitting at other tables were forming images of arguing, fighting, strangling or running them over with their cars, although their faces showed no signs of hatred, just boredom.

"What would people think if I walked to a table and said to a woman- "you know madam your husband sees himself on the beach in the Caribbean with the lady sitting next to you" or to the man at the far end -"you know, the man you are talking to has sold you a car that won't last till Easter and he is proud of himself.?"

She did not join the line on the floor with Auntie Siobhan, it was far too difficult for her capabilities in Greek dances so far.

As Uncle Yorgi was singing, with all his heart and emotions, she noted that some of the thoughts in the minds of the audience were calming down, the hateful images tended to vanish and gradually, she was happy to see that some had blue halos above their heads. She could not help thinking that the music must have had a magical effect, providing people were willing to surrender to it. The people were all different, some very sad but smiling nevertheless, others genuinely happy- rich and poor, young and poor- but for this particular handful of seconds, in tune, moved by the voice of Uncle Yorgi. Pauline could see that they were brushing aside their first thoughts to share the same feelings of melancholy and tenderness. "Just like that?" she wondered. "As if we receive images in our minds the way we receive rain or snow on our noses. Can we choose what we want to think, then, and build a barrier against images from the outside, the same way we put earphones on so as to listen only to the music we want to play on an MP4? Perhaps, people who can't build barriers against spurious thoughts, who don't have a firewall to protect their brains against spam are more fragile?

Something to discuss with her father.

For once, the family was complete, since Uncle Yorgi and Auntie Siobhan had brought their three children, not only Ruby, who had caught Pauline in the middle of a petits yiyis trip, but also their two tall sons, Joe and Mat. They were in their late teens, over 1 m 92, perhaps even 1 m 95 for Joe, the second son. They look as Greek as I look French, she thought. They could have replaced the tall actor Benedict Cumberbach who played Sherlock Holmes in the latest BBC series.

Hang on a minute, she said to herself, if Ruby is an advanced Rescuer- which she had more or less admitted- what about her older brothers?

As if he had read her mind, Joe, Mat's younger brother, and probably the only red-haired Greek on the island, placed his hand on Pauline's forearm and said, with a broad smile- "Mat has just completed his truck driving licence and is going to the North of Europe at the end of January."

"Fantastic, he will be able to bring the....." she started and Joe placed a finger on his mouth, winking at her.

That answered one question, Ruby's brothers were at least aware of the Rescuers, and she could imagine Mat teaming up with Jas on trips from Paris to Zakynthos with a truck load of Refugees.

But would it be the first time? If so, why had they waited so long? Perhaps the number of Refugees had outgrown the capacity of the Rescuers... Perhaps the spread of obnoxious oil had been a disaster.

She decided to pry a little: "A lot of olive oil is shipped from the island to many countries, in Europe'" she said matter-of-factly. Mat, who had returned from the line dancing overheard her.

"Yes, but sadly, some people tamper with it" he commented, as if to let her carry on.

She wanted to talk about the contaminated oil. She wanted to know who poisoned it. She had seen recently on French TV that some people in Austria had added anti-freeze liquid, normally used for cars in cold Austrian winters, to the oil to sell larger quantities and make more money with little effort. They had been caught eventually, but the effects had been devastating.

She assumed that poisoned oil helped create bad thoughts- particularly in people who were already inclined that way- acting like an amplifier, a booster.

And now, who was fighting against the poisoners, rescuers of Higher Grade, like Ruby and her brothers? What could they do? More and more oil arrived daily in restaurants and supermarkets so the fight was ongoing.

"You are absolutely right" Mat said, smiling, as if he had heard the latest words she had pronounced in her head.

Pauline thought, I must be careful if he can read my mind, at the same time trying to fight it so as to keep her mind blank.

"Don't worry, we are on the same side, and with time, you can learn to build a shield, like a scrambler against mobile phones in military compounds or prisons".

Against her free will, she wondered whether she could read his mind, as well, or in fact anybody's mind. She could not only see coloured halos produced by complete strangers unexpectedly, but also at will, in a controlled way, as she drove her petits yiyis.

"Yes, you will, but it takes time, be patient," answered Joe, winking at his brother.

Chapter Seventeen

The hopper plane from Zakynthos to Athens took only forty minutes and Pauline already felt sad, leaving this island. A few seconds after taking off, the plane was above Turtle Island and she could imagine that in the next few weeks Jas, the transporter and Mat, Uncle Yorgi's oldest son, would bring as many Refugees there as they could. She was trying to calculate how many abandoned petits yiyis could be placed on a tray, filled with compost and covered with sawdust. Would Jas transport them for free? Probably. And of course, he would bring delicatessen food and wines for the expats.

After a couple of hours in Athens airport, surrounded by mountains, she took her second plane, this time, for Paris, where she would land 3 hours later, and where it would be at least ten degrees colder...

The plane was flying above the clouds, real ones, she hoped, because if they were composed of shards of glass filled with angry faces, now was the ideal time to get rid of her and there would have been nothing, or not a lot, to prevent them from doing so.

She let her mind wander from one passenger's head to another and discovered that without focusing too much, she could see a colour form on top of their heads, changing shapes and sometimes turning into other colours. There must be a code to interpret these visions she thought. Like everything in this world, you must learn to understand. She couldn't wait to be taken to a

Higher Grade, like Ruby, or even better, Joe or especially Mat.

What about Uncle Yorgi and the other adults, what about her father, how did they fit in? There were so many unanswered questions. It seemed that each time she opened a door, she found a corridor or a path, leading to even more paths, each time with something to learn, to take on board, and raising new questions that she did not have at the start.

She dozed off and woke up half an hour before landing. She needed to be clear in her mind: first organise the "Great Migration" of the Refugees, secondly find out whether she and her friends could rescue other Refugees hiding in Paris or its outskirts, and thirdly, and ideally, set up a regular scheme of repatriation to Turtle Island.

The poisoned oil, used by the Angries to wipe out the Rainlights, was a major source of concern.

She was running out of inspiration and could not wait to have a brainstorming session with her friends.

She had taken many photos of the island of Zakynthos, with the tablet that her father had given her, and of various spots, like Turtle Island the beach of Alykes, where the children had seen the Spheres, and of the ferry port, where hopefully thousands of rescued petits yiyis could soon disembark.

Her father was waiting for her at Roissy Charles-de-Gaulle airport, with the old car he had had for over twenty years, a classic car he had used in the past for driving around Europe. Getting to their flat by the Moulin-Rouge took the best part of an hour, which was not too bad. She was very excited to tell her father about her first time dancing the Zeibekiko. And after the usual chit-chat about her holiday, she decided to come clean about what she had experienced over the last few weeks. As she was talking, she had the impression that her father was walking alongside her on one of the paths she had begun to see, as if to put images on her feelings, when she was going from one question to an answer. When she mentioned her mother's visits in the green whirl pool, he did not flinch and she felt that they were both walking on this path in this parallel world, her father grabbing hold of her hand, as if he feared she might fall into the ditch.

She continued her story, about the vision of the spheres, of people's minds, of colours forming above their heads.

For a moment, she closed her eyes. Her father had not said a word, concentrating on the traffic. She could see them both walking up a path leading to an old castle. They arrived at the drawbridge, which was still upright and thus needed to be lowered.

"Not yet." her father whispered softly, putting the brakes on at the traffic lights, and also on her mind-travelling. She opened her eyes, a little unhappy that all these grown-ups were killjoys.

***

"Anybody have a brilliant idea?" Pauline asked her friends, together once again in her father's flat.

"As we are beginners," Sarah ventured, "the signs must be reasonably easy to find, otherwise, we would already be admitted to the higher grade Ruby is in."

"It's probably staring us in the face!" Aurelio said. "Let's look at a map of Paris."

Pauline had pinned an old looking map of the French capital on the wall which was on the left-hand side when entering the flat. The six children walked a few paces and were scrutinising the two-by-one-metre-or-so map.

"With four thousands streets, it may take years to comb them!" Nafissatou exclaimed.

"There might hundreds of places where abandoned petits yiyis are waiting, perhaps some of them are even ..." Fatima said.

"We must find a kind of beacon, or signpost!" Zhi Ruo stated.

"Something obvious, but not too obvious, otherwise the Angries can find them and destroy them ..." Sarah continued

"Or even poison them and return them to healthy groups hiding in shelters, in order to contaminate them!" Nafissatou added.

"That would be really vicious..." Aurelio commented.

"And even if they look like the lights on but there's nobody home, it may be within the realm of their accomplishments!" Nafissatou exclaimed joyfully.

"What about the Tour Eiffel?" Sarah asked.

"What about it?" Fatima replied.

"Yes, it throws a light, all around Paris, like a light-house off a dangerous shore..." Pauline said.

"Perhaps, a ray of a special colour lingers on various districts, streets even, and points out hiding places for

Refugees, for the healthier to carry the wounded, to safety?" Fatima ventured.

"This is great!" Zhi Ruo resumed.

"But who operates the projector on the third floor of the Tour Eiffel?" Nafissatou asked.

"Perhaps petits yiyis like us, take turns, take shifts, controlled by more advanced Rescuers ..."Aurelio commented.

They all remembered seeing rays of different colours drawing circles over the streets of Paris, all the year round, sometimes the rays would hit the boundaries of Paris with the suburbs, others, they hit the ground a few hundred metres away.

"Right, let's assume that the Tour Eiffel can lead us, and this remains to be proven..." Pauline stated again. "We need to be able to interpret the meaning of the colours and to be fast enough to see what streets they hit."

"We know that the code must be breakable by beginners like us, but still hard enough to escape the Angries..." Fatima added. "So perhaps it's a combination of the rays of colour and ... the names of the streets, of places, of monuments."

Another long silence.

"Yes," Zhi Ruo said, "suppose a ray of a given colour, which we need to recognise, falls onto a district or a block of streets, we could proceed by elimination and narrow our research down to a couple of streets."

"Perhaps the colour is intense or changes and dwells on a spot, to guide the abandoned milk petits yiyis," Aurelio ventured.

"But where are they hiding as they wait for a sign?" Nafissatou asked.

"There are many trees in Paris, in all the wider streets, and there are metal grids at their feet. Ideal for them to hide for a short while." Zhi Ruo replied.

They all looked at each other.

"Fancy a little trip tonight?" Pauline asked, with a broad smile.

***

"I suggest that we assume six different positions," Pauline said, "pointing at the map of Paris on the wall, Nafissatou in the North West, Aurelio in the North in the centre, Zhi Ruo in the North East, Fatima in the South East, me in the South in the centre and Sarah in the South West, that way we can all follow the beams of the Tour Eiffel and as soon we think we've got something, we notify the others and we regroup."

They nodded, opened the skylight and off went the little V-shaped squadrons, almost like professional drones now.

They were all at their posts, perched on the top of a church or building, securing an unimpeded view of the beam projected from the third floor of the Tour Eiffel.

Rays of blue, green, yellow, red, orange, violet, purple, and white were hitting the streets in turn, sometimes drawing lines, going up and down avenues, then a little to the right, or to the left, briefly, always high enough so as not to blind the drivers

"Pauline," Zhi Ruo said with her eyes closed, from the South West border of Paris "there is a <u>yellow</u> beam which was coming from my right, it paused and is going back towards you."

"I can see it too, "Fatima added, who was positioned in the South West. "There must be something in the South Centre."

Pauline could now see a yellow beam pausing above the Place d'Italie and descending gently down Avenue de Choisy, swiftly turning right towards the Boulevard Massena, suddenly red flashing, then turning green, then going right and upwards, to the Avenue d'Italie, following the same pattern, then swiftly turning white and moving away to the East and far to the West, and anticlockwise.

"So far, "Aurelio said from his central position in the North of Paris, "it has been the only proper geographical pattern, a triangle."

"Let's try it" Pauline invited them to join her above the Place d'Italie. This Square marks the beginning of the two China Towns in Paris, with more than 50,000 inhabitants in an area of the size of a few football pitches, so finding Refugees would be like looking for a needle in a haystack.

"Sarah and I will go up and down Avenue de Choisy, Fatima and Zhi Ruo up and down Boulevard Massena, while Nafissatou and Aurelio go up and down Avenue d'Italie," Pauline said.

Would it be too easy, she thought briefly, if red was for stop, amber for caution, green to go-ahead? But, if it was a test, perhaps they ought to start simply.

They flew up and down a few times, without success. Perhaps they would not witness a mass migration of scared petits yiyis tonight, perhaps they were being tested for their ability to find another hiding place, like the one Pauline had been taken to at the very beginning of her adventures.

"Think," she said to herself, "there must be a clue, one you can interpret."

There were half a dozen streets parallel to the Boulevard Massena, with names of past politicians or inventors, nothing that rang a bell. There was a hospital, but there again, no, Pauline drew a blank. All of a sudden, she had a hunch.

"Look," she said to her friends, "there is a church at the bottom of Avenue de Choisy." she was getting very excited. "It's name is Saint Hippolyte, in Greek it would be Agios Hippolytos and it means one who like horses, like in the movie the Horse Whisperer, it's a Greek name, you understand? As if someone from Zakynthos or connected with Zakynthos were guiding me, and you."

They were now hovering above the church and little by little they could see petits yiyis coming from under the metal grids around the trees of Avenue de Choisy, dozens, then hundreds, some flying faintly, other stronger yiyis helping those who had been deprived of food and attention for a longer time.

There was a basement at the other end of the church, away from the street.

There was no sign of the Clouds.

The children could see a long procession of petits yiyis entering the basement of Saint Hippolyte Church. Yes, their assumptions had been right…

"Time to introduce ourselves, don't you think?" asked Pauline, starting the descent towards the basement.

Chapter Eighteen

"How is Aurelio doing with the bullies?" Pauline asked Zhi Ruo in the school courtyard, during the morning intermission.

"Well, so far they have ignored him and found other little boys, even more vulnerable. But Aurelio has been a good student in martial arts while you were in Greece!" A Tai-Chi Master in the making she replied joyfully. "I told him the secret of the shortcut to success," she added, with a wink.

"Really?" Pauline asked.

"Yes, practice, practice and practice again!" she answered. "In fact, I taught him a few defensive moves, only a couple, and asked him to repeat them many times over, breathing in slowly when gathering momentum and then breathing out with power when striking the air, as if pushing waves, with his palm open like a tiger or his fingers extended like a snake. Just these, but I think he's good enough, especially if he can demonstrate patience, then I shall take him to the next stage."

"How old were when you started to learn?" Pauline inquired.

"Probably as soon as I could stand up and walk..."

"Well, it's a bit like what we are experiencing. We were led to discover a bit, then to act a bit, then to discover a little bit more and to act a little bit more" Pauline thought aloud.

"Look!" Nafissatou exclaimed, "Fabien, the head bully has brought his nunchaku!"

Pauline had seen this instrument in a few "Kung-Fu video games": two pieces of wood, or metal, linked by a cord or a chain, and the artist would hold onto one piece then catch the other behind his neck, his shoulder, or his leg, faster and faster, delivering blows by simply aiming the free piece into the body of an opponent, which could be devastatingly harmful.

Fabien assumed the position of a ninja fighter and was using his nunchaku away from the view of a teacher, who would confiscate it. His friends were mesmerised, Fabien was manipulating his nunchaku faster and faster, until he caught sight of Aurelio lost in his day-dreaming, walking towards Pauline and her friends, Fabien felt that his moment of glory was offered on a tray and tip toed towards the young unsuspecting boy, holding his nunchaku behind his back. He stopped in front of Aurelio, barring his way and starting to juggle. Aurelio looked panicked for a fleeting second, then met the reassuring eyes of Zhi Ruo. He did not flee, as Fabien expected. Instead, he planted his feet firmly onto the ground, and started to breathe in and out, gently, while Fabien seemed to juggle faster and faster, with an angry grin on his face, coming closer and closer towards Aurelio, who had his arms in front of his chest, rotating his wrists gently.

This had the effect of increasing Fabien's hostility, now juggling really fast, throwing his nunchaku behind his back and round his belly. As one piece was climbing in front of his face, Aurelio pushed his palms swiftly in front of him, as if pushing waves with all his strength, breathing out in a single powerful sigh. He did not touch the nunchaku, but the air displaced the piece of wood, moving it into Fabien's face. Fabien let out a great ouch, and dropped his instrument, out for the count. His friends were splitting their sides laughing, which proved even more humiliating.

Aurelio was still in front of him, waiting for any encore, but Fabien picked up his nunchaku and walked away, booed off by a no-longer supporting crowd.

The five girls who had been standing by all along, exchanged knowing glances.

***

"What are we going to do next?" Fatima asked in Pauline's flat, during their usual general meeting.

"Jas and Mat are coming in three weeks, with a truck," Pauline replied. "In the meantime we need to find as many hiding places as we can."

"And to keep watch!" Sarah added.

"Shouldn't we bring them all to a single place?" Fatima continued.

They remained silent for a while, weighing the pros and cons.

"Obviously, if we find a few more Refugees camps, it may be easier to load them in one go onto the truck," Zhi Ruo commented.

"We have managed not to lose any abandoned petit yiyis so far and we don't want to push our luck" Aurelio ventured.

"They will all be together in the truck and for a long journey. There are about 1300 km from Paris to Ancona, then 24 hours on a ferry, to Patras, in Greece, then one hour or so to Killini, another ferry, for another hour, when they arrive on the island of Zakynthos then twenty minutes to Turtle Island. That gives plenty of time for the Clouds to attack- nearly two days!" Pauline exclaimed.

"We must find a way of protecting them. Clouds may surround the truck on the motorway and cause an accident," Nafissatou started.

Pauline flinched. Was that what had happened to her mother? She did not know any details so perhaps.

"You have seen what happened between Fabien, the chief school bully, and Aurelio?" Zhi Ruo started. They nodded. "The more Fabien was getting angry, the more obvious it became he was going to fail."

They were all trying to figure out how they could challenge the Clouds and lead to them into making multiple fatal mistakes.

"We have three weeks to build a suitable defensive tactic," Zhi Ruo concluded.

***

Pauline kept thinking about her mother's accident since her discussion with her friends. Had she been killed by the clouds, had she sacrificed herself, as a decoy, while other rescuers were bringing Refugees to a place of safety, in the mountains?

She had another hunch. The mountains? Yes, it was in the Alps, near Switzerland, in the village where several ancestors of her father had been born over the centuries.

Actually, saying to herself, Jas and Mat will be driving through the Alps, near Aix-les-Bains and then take the Mont-Blanc Tunnel, where her mother had the accident. Perhaps there was another sanctuary there and Jas and Mat could collect another bunch. But how can we get in touch with these abandoned petits yiyis in the Alps, 500 km away, at least? There is not much time to the end of the month.

At that moment, a green whirl pool formed in her bedroom, its base barely touching the floor. For once, she had not used her petits yiyis, she had just conjured up her mother's image, picturing her in her car, in the Mont-Blanc Tunnel, perhaps the intensity of her concentration had dialled a number in the other world, she thought.

"Good evening mein Schatz!" she heard her mother say.

Pauline leapt onto the floor and stopped short of the green whirl pool.

"Mutti! I miss you so much!" the young girl exclaimed, with tears starting to trickle down her cheeks.

Her mother seemed to hesitate for a moment, moving her head sideways as if looking for approval from someone.

"Komm mal rein (Come on in)," she said to Pauline, who jumped in, feeling the warmth of her mother just like she remembered, tall and strong, but now, out of reach - or perhaps not.

Her mother lifted her up and said softly: "close your eyes, Pauline!"

She could feel an acceleration, as if they were on the underground and the speed was increasing indefinitely, then they slowed down and her mother dropped her gently on the grass. She opened her eyes and saw valleys with daisies, quiet lakes, hardly any wind around, birds chirping. She was standing opposite her mother and threw her arms around her.

"I would like to stay here, with you, forever!" she said. "Is it where you live now?"

"Yes," her mother replied, "in a way."

"Is it what we call Paradise?" Pauline asked, filled with hope.

"No, it's just another world of existence- more permanent - but" and she stopped.

Not again! Pauline thought. How come no one can give me a full explanation whenever I ask a simple question?

"Because your questions can never be answered simply!" her mother replied, as if reading her mind. "Just try to enjoy the moment- you and your friends have passed all the tests so far, but if you go too fast, you may fail and all your training will have been in vain."

Pauline felt a bit frustrated.

"Next year you will go to college, right?"

"Yes, I know, but."

"Could you follow the lessons of next year at this very minute?"

Pauline let her mind wander: "Probably not?"

"Because you need to lay firm foundations first, in maths, history, grammar, and so on, and only then can you build a ground floor, and then a first floor, slowly and steadily."

So Pauline was right, they had been tested. She had thousands of questions to pose to her mother such as: -why her, and why her friends, Nafissatou, Zhi Ruo, Fatima, Sarah and Aurelio. What did Ruby and her brothers Mat and Joe know that Pauline and her friends did not? What did the adults, Uncle Yorgi, Auntie Siobhan, Jas and, especially her father, know that they had all refused to tell Pauline? What was the meaning of the Spheres which had appeared off the shore of Alykes, where each child could see herself and himself grow up and choose to stay as a Rainlight or join the Angries?" She had so many others as well. But she thought better of asking more, knowing that she would be told to bide her time.

"Knowledge always sticks better if you acquire a lot of it on your own" her mother said. "You will see, you will feel attracted by a sort of door whenever you are ready to enter and when you are ready to understand and to progress, otherwise, it would be like force-feeding a goose."

However much she resented it, Pauline had to admit that her mother was right.

"So we have discovered a hiding place for the abandoned petits yiyis in the basement of Saint Hippolyte Church, on Avenue de Choisy, in the South centre of Paris, because we followed the light projected from the Tour Eiffel. I suppose the next test will be more difficult, and so on."

"Yes" her mother paused, "you must continue to be a Learner, until such time as you can become a Teacher."

Pauline felt dizzy, as if a gigantic wave of air were pushing her backwards and forwards. "Don't worry, you are doing remarkably well" Her mother lifted her in her arms again. Time to go back to the Slow World she whispered.

Seeing that tears were forming in her daughter's eyes, she hastened to add. "You know now that we are neighbours"

Chapter Nineteen

"Why a Slow World?" Pauline was wondering in her bed. She had fallen asleep quite quickly, but now, in the darkness of the night, with the lights of the city throwing timid rays through the little turn-and-tilt window in the roof, she found it hard to go to sleep again. Obviously, she felt comforted that she could meet with her mother again anytime she wanted to, or almost, she was not sure yet. Had she had a vision of the landscapes, the wind, the castle on the hill, or had it simply been her mother talking to her? This had led her to think that she could come and go between two worlds. But why did she use the expression Slow World? How many worlds were there? Did they all look the same, but with doors, and gateways, as she had seen in some supermarkets in Paris, where two sections were linked by a glass corridor situated above the street level, so that customers did not need to come out and get wet from the rain in order to browse through the various departments?

"If I, or my friends, my father and the people I see around me, live in a slow world then who lives in a fast world, and are there other names to depict other sorts of worlds? Do we all have the same shapes, the same sizes, the same colours? Do we breathe the same air? Could she control her petits yiyis in other worlds as well?"

Pauline was wondering about the possibility of moving faster, like using a motorway or a speeding bus, or a high speed train, but they needed to move faster than the Clouds. Perhaps she and the children could use the Faster World to escape the Clouds and reappear safely, far away, with the Refugees?

But then, where did the petits yiyis fit in? Were they like keys, or like jacks that you plug in to a wall socket to charge a tablet?

And what about her father, would he meet with her mother as well? Was there a reason why she had to leave this world? All over again, she was cautioned to be patient, but it was frustrating.

As if quoting from memory she remembered her father saying "the mysteries of nature are not to be unfolded to all who seek her shrine, but only to the strong in faith and the humble in spirit". A sentence that flew right up over her head, but she understood that it was tinted with wisdom.

"What does it mean?" she had asked, fearing that the answer would be even more confusing.

"I once heard a lawyer say that in court, you should never ask a question if you don't know the answer!' he had replied. Then, seeing the puzzled look on Pauline's face, he had added: -"Try to discover first by yourself, then seek for confirmation, and check again, otherwise, it's a waste of time and you will be even more lost! In other words, learn slowly, like a cow chewing grass, ruminating and digesting gradually!"

***

"What do they add to the oil to poison it?" Pauline asked her friend during their regular academic session. They had all seen scandals on TV or on the Internet where companies cut corners by adding cheaper ingredients to foodstuffs with dreadful consequences, like babies ending up in hospital.

"We need to know what is added" Fatima stated.

"Or removed" Aurelio commented.

"Indeed," Zhi Ruo resumed, "we know that oil from pure trees acts like a sweet treatment, promoting nice actions or simply rewarding good deeds, whereas the poisoned oil triggers wrong-doing in people who are more vulnerable…"

"Pauline has told us about her vision of good thoughts being captured by trees, and being recorded by them" Nafissatou ventured, then he paused. "What if the trees work both ways?"

She saw the gigantic question mark on her friends' faces. As images formed in her mind, she continued: - "Suppose that the trees absorb the positive, the kind images, the gentle thoughts we have for others, the love we give"

"Yes?" her friends replied in unison.

"Perhaps, they also capture the opposite, the negative thoughts, the images filled with hatred, the anger we have for others, our desire to hurt others" she concluded.

"Then they reject all these and throw them away, as we throw away refuse in the chute to be collected by garbage trucks?" Pauline ventured.

"Right," Aurelio stepped in, "but then where do they reject the refuse?"

"And how does it end up in the oil?" Fatima wondered.

"Perhaps, the trees try to recycle it, to reduce its toxicity and lock up these harmful thoughts in leaves, which fall, become dead leaves and turn into weeds," Sarah proposed. "We have all seen how weeds spread easily, far more easily than vegetables or flowers."

"Hang on," Nafissatou intervened, "if you are right the Refugees in the Jardin des Plantes are at risk, they may become contaminated and if we take them to the island of Zakynthos, they may in turn contaminate all the others, like a flu virus!"

They all went silent.

"Yes," Pauline resumed, "from the Clouds that would be a diabolical plan! Let's collect the Refugees, which were once pure milk petits yiyis and we, thinking that we have rescued them, might have exposed them to a greater danger if the trees in the tropical greenhouse do their job and recycle bad thoughts."

"We may have poisoned them!" Fatima exclaimed.

"Don't be alarmed!" Zhi Ruo rushed to say, "every poison has an antidote, we just need to find it!'

***

The six children met up again, later, that night and sent their V-shaped squadrons to the tropical garden in the Jardin des Plantes, where they had hidden the Refugees, waiting for Jason and Mat to come all the way from Zakynthos with a truck to collect them.

"It's just as well that we left the other group of Refugees in the basement of Saint Hippolyte Church, in case the first group has been poisoned," Nafissatou said.

"Zhi Ruo is our medical expert," Pauline said, a little tongue-in-cheek, "let's keep watch all around the greenhouse and wait for her report."

Zhi Ruo had displayed a vast knowledge about plants and their properties while talking to the others during their Tai-Chi exercises. She pointed out that each of the basic eighteen hand movements was beneficial for certain muscles, certain organs, as preventive measures, and in that case, none of the members of the group would contemplate dialling 01 53 94 94 94 for an emergency medical consultation.

Zhi Ruo's petits yiyis flew into the greenhouse. She could not put her smallest yiyi on it, but something did not feel right. It was unusually calm, without any wind, as if the plants had stopped vibrating and were decaying.

She sent her reconnaissance squad to the place where they had left the Refugees.

Weeds had grown fast and were stinking. She could see a few blackened spots emerging from the soil, as if the Refugees were gasping for air.

"What can I do?" she asked herself. Suddenly, she saw a couple of Shadows hugging the window panes, just Shadows, alone, without human. She hid her petits yiyis under a palm leaf and watched the Shadows go from one flower bed to the next.

"Where are they going, what are they doing?" she wanted to know. They didn't speak, but the closer they came, the stronger the stench. Were they part of the

Clouds, were they sent by the Angries? Perhaps the Angries, or some of them, instead of sending their wisdom petits yiyis, sent their Shadows like drones.

She moved her petits yiyis to the side and saw that Shadows were rising from the soil.

"It's not looking good" she said to her friends. "I think that the Refugees are more in danger than we thought!" She told them about the stench and the Shadows, rising from the soil, surely from the decomposing weeds, the weeds that were produced by the dead leaves and nourished by the negative images captured by the trees.

"What if the Shadows grew even faster in the presence of abandoned petits yiyis?" Aurelio said.

"Evil creatures breeding on feeble good creatures!" Sarah exclaimed.

"The Refugees are defenceless, so they can't resist the weeds and are gradually being stifled" Nafissatou added.

"Let's go back, we need to think" Pauline said, regretfully. "There's nothing we can do right now."

A few minutes later, the petits yiyis reconnected to the children's feet and Zhi Ruo could recount in detail what she had seen.

"So," Pauline stated, "we now know that the Clouds are not our sole enemies, we also have to face the Shadows."

"Both stink like rotten eggs, so it should be easy to smell their presence!" Aurelio said, as if to find a reason for remaining optimistic.

"This could explain why the Refugees in the South of Paris sought shelter in a basement, and not in a park, where they would be more vulnerable to weeds, and the Shadows!" Fatima thought aloud.

"When they are not chased by the Clouds" Sarah added.

"Well so far we have found ways of fighting the Clouds," Pauline resumed. "Everything in nature has a weak point, an Achilles' heel, as they say in Greece."

"The Shadows are born from weeds, right?" Nafissatou started. "Remove the weeds and you prevent the Shadows from growing!"

"But the Refugees need soil for protection!" Aurelio commented.

"They are in danger in the soil though" Sarah continued, "unless…

We can find a way of keeping them in the soil and at the same time, prevent the development of weeds" Fatima added.

"Let's go back to the very basics," Pauline said, "everything seems to be linked to the olive tree, right?"

The other children nodded.

"We know that olive oil is sometimes poisoned to spread or to increase evil, right again?"

They were all in agreement.

"So, can you see where I'm coming from?"

"The antidote may be pure oil from Zakynthos. Perhaps if we spray it on the soil where the Refugees are hiding the weeds will disintegrate and become harmless," Nafissatou exclaimed after a long pause.

"With more than two million olive trees over there, we might have a job for life!" Aurelio exclaimed.

"Indeed, and if I remember correctly, Uncle Yorgi said they produce more than twenty million litres per year!"

"Enough to spray a few green spaces and parks all over the world!" Sarah exclaimed.

For a fleeting moment, Pauline wondered whether this was not what Ruby and more advanced Rescuers were doing, but she put it in a corner of a mind, to think about it later.

"And to do all this, without the Clouds following us!" Zhi Ruo said. "And what do we know about the Shadows? I saw them moving. Were they controlled? What do they do?"

"Perhaps we can build a trap for the Shadows?" Aurelio asked.

"Or better still" Pauline said, smiling, "we can try to follow them."

"Yes, I like that!" Zhi Ruo, "the hunted becomes the hunter!"

Chapter Twenty

Once again, Pauline had the impression that she was being taken on a stroll with invisible hands. Look, she said to herself the following day, don't you find it odd that Auntie Siobhan gave you two bottles of the pure olive oil from Zakynthos, supposedly to use for cooking, when she knows that my father only cooks on rare occasions?"

So, she called her friends to tell them about her about her cunning plan.

The six friends gathered and held hands again but this time, with a slight difference. Pauline had prepared a bath for their petits yiyis, a small plastic tub filled with half a bottle of the oil offered by Auntie Siobhan.

The children let their toes dive into it and hoped that Pauline's hunch was not a craze.

The petits yiyis, thus purified, took off from the flat and flew towards the Jardin des Plantes. Arriving at the heavy gate, Pauline let Zhi Ruo's squad through first, since she was the one who had seen the Shadows the night before. It was not too long before the Tai Chi Master smelled the nauseating odour of the intruders. She motioned her followers towards the flower beds where the Refugees were hiding, probably holding their breath so as not to be stifled by the stench diffused by the Shadows, who had been sent by the Angries to destroy the Refugees, or to absorb their energy, who knows.

The sixty petits yiyis started to shake off the oil, with which they had been impregnated, onto the flower beds. Soon little trickles of oil from the island of Uncle Yorgi and Auntie Siobhan fell onto the soil, generating golden sparks and multiplying infinitely, immediately coating the emerging parts of the Refugees, who gradually began to cicada at the joy of surviving their ordeal.

Attracted by the growing chirping-like sounds, Shadows hovered across from the far end of the tropical greenhouse. Zhi Ruo was the closest and had been the first to drop the revitalising nectar onto the weak petits yiyis in the soil, but kept a little at the tip of each of her ten little petits yiyis, which were soon to become little daggers . They went through the first Shadow, and in Pauline's flat, where she was controlling her little weapons remotely like the other 5 friends, she felt like throwing up. She pierced the first Shadow several times and it started to decompose and vanish into the night.

Aurelio was behind her and attacked the second Shadow, with the same result. The other Shadows, apparently not so pleased at the demise of their accomplices, rushed to their rescue. Nafissatou and Fatima came to help and drilled a couple, flying around and though them. Pauline and Sarah were still shaking off their oil to make sure that all the poor Refugees had enough nourishment to recover from their recent starvation. Now they joined the squad of little snipers.

It now looked like the beginning of a rugby match with the All Blacks about to do the Haka, the dance that the New Zealand team performs in front of the opposing team in order to put fear into them. Pauline's team was facing a dozen Shadows, stinking like a fish left to rot outside a closed restaurant.

146

"Let's act fast, otherwise we shall be beaten!" she exclaimed. So the six V-shaped squads went for it, the friends inhaling air in Pauline's flat to gather power, and sending it to their petits yiyis with their minds, then breathing out with the maximum strength they could, to push waves of air towards the Shadows. The latter did not expect the confrontation and reeled back. Zhi Ruo was the first to come closer and the others followed, making gushes of air again and again. They still had a few drops of oil, which combined with the blasts of air, knocked out most of the Shadows. Some stank more than others and were consequently more resistant.

"You can't stop a truck with a match stick," Zhi Ruo said. "Let's split in two groups of three, as I showed you the other day, in our self-defence class."

So, Zhi Ruo led a group composed of Fatima and Aurelio, while Pauline flew to the other side of the tropical greenhouse with Nafissatou and Sarah.

The 4 big, reeking Shadows still standing seemed to pause and think, then two decided to chase the trio led by Zhi Ruo and the other two went for Pauline and her two friends.

Seeing that the Shadows were following them, both trios started to accelerate, zigzag and then made an about-turn, one team of three on the right of the central alley, the other, coming in the opposite direction, on the left side. Then, approaching a big tall tree, Zhi Ruo crossed the alley quickly, ducking just before colliding with Pauline's team, flying towards them at full speed.

The Shadows, blinded by their will to do harm, did not have the time to adjust their trajectory and bumped into each other head on, falling to the ground, where some of the Refugees emerged from the soil and happily projected a few tiny drops of the oil they had received a few minutes ago, on the vanquished Shadows.

"That was a narrow escape!" Pauline said, after the petits yiyis had re-joined their respective owners in her flat.

"Let's hope that Mat and Jas won't be too long!" Fatima said. "We may not be so lucky next time."

***

"Papa, how do you know if our olive oil has been poisoned?" Pauline asked the following Sunday morning. She realised that she had said OUR olive oil, as if she were part of the production team in Zakynthos, but in a small way, she was.

Her father scratched his chin for a few seconds then replied: "I am going to show you."

They took the bus, and forty minutes later arrived at Place d'Italie, only a few hundred metres from Saint Hippolyte Church, at the bottom of Avenue de Choisy, where a group of Refugees were also waiting for a means of transport to be taken to more clement climates.

"Let's walk a bit," he said to Pauline. So they walked the Avenue des Gobelins and after ten minutes arrived at Rue Mouffetard.

"I know!" she exclaimed joyfully, "we are going to have lunch at Le Cretois!" It was a Greek restaurant where her father had been a regular visitor for decades.

When they entered, her father gave a hug to the owner and the waiters, as the custom goes in Greece. Only recently had Pauline and her father started to go back there. It was too painful during the first few months after her mother died.

Still, her father had said nothing to satisfy her curiosity, "How do you know if oil is poisoned?"

As her father was ordering the meal, Pauline was trying to focus hard to catch what her father and the owner were saying, very fast.

What was her father up to? He had not spoken at all about the poisonous oil, or rather, how pure oil could be poisoned and by whom? She suspected that weeds would be added somewhere along the production line, perhaps during the pressing stage or the bottling process or, more likely, when barrels were left unattended on a ferry on its way to the continent. But how did you recognise that supposedly pure oil was in fact some kind of poison? And most of all, what were the effects on people?

Two couples entered the restaurant: a bald guy who looked a little like the advert for Mr Muscle, and his wife, whose face reminded Pauline of a goose in a cartoon, then the second, the man, a born leader, ordering people around and his giggling wife following, with an expensive would-be-Hollywood-star hair style.

Pauline's father lit up with joy. He winked at one of the waiters, who was standing idly by until the two couples had sat down.

"This is on the house, while you peruse the menu at leisure," said the waiter after a few seconds, bringing a large dish of sliced bread with tomatoes, capers, feta (Greek cheese) and a little oil.

'This is our special oil, from the island of Sapulakras, spread it on your bruschettas, and the more you spread the sweeter they will taste" he commented.

The two men began to pour the oil profusely on the slices of bread.

The leader of the pack, the husband of the giggling lady, was explaining how business at his bank had never been so prosperous.

"Can you read their minds?" Pauline's father asked her.

Indeed, she saw that the goose-looking lady was reminiscing about when she was young, dreaming of becoming a danseuse étoile (First Dancer) in the Opéra de Paris, resenting the fact that her husband, with the bald head and eyes spaced wide apart, had compelled her to stop to breed their two spoiled girls.

Her husband was twenty years in the past, trying to set up his own building contracting business, that he had packed in because he did not have the courage to take risks and his wife, as if to retaliate, was keeping him under the thumb.

Then Pauline shifted to the giggling lady's mind. Indeed, every three words she heard, she emitted a giggle. In her day-dream, she remembered the days when she wanted to become the new Madonna, but then one day, on holiday in the South of France, on a coach tour, as she started to sing "la isla bonita" with all her heart, body and soul, she saw seagulls diving into the window panes of the coach, to try and shush her.

Finally, the insurance broker. He had wanted to become the Président de la République, but had to settle for a very well paid job in a bank on the Champs-Elysées.

"They all seem very sad…" Pauline said to her father.

"Wait a little…" her father added, winking at the waiter.

The latter rushed gently to their table and said "Please allow me" spraying a few large drops of oil onto their slices of bread.

As they continued to eat, the pictures in their minds were really turning sour and the more they added oil from Sapulakras, the more Pauline could see dreadful images:- the goose-lady started to look at her husband while clutching her knife, as if to plant the blade in his heart, Mr Muscle's jaws were trembling, as if he were about to punch his wife in the nose and the giggling lady was laughing louder and louder, with anger-filled eyes at her husband, wishing he would rake in more money.

Only the insurance broker seemed unaffected by the oil from the island of Sapulakras, except perhaps for a few jokes about people he humiliated off and on at work.

The waiter poured some more oil and Pauline could see that three of them were about to cause a blood bath.

"Papa, arête (daddy, stop it), they are going to kill each other."

Her father raised his hand to his forehead, as if to ask a question and the waiter walked back to the table of the two couples.*

"Excuse me, I think I gave you the wrong bottle, it may be off and this one is on the house. Please accept our apologies!" He removed the oil from Sapulakras (an island which never existed anyway) and replaced it with pure virgin oil from Zakynthos, with which he dowsed the pieces of bread remaining on their plates.

As if by a miracle, attitudes changed within a few dozen seconds: the goose lady went back to her dreams of the past, Mr Muscle was again glued to the words of the insurance broker, and the giggling lady was back in her world of 'France's got talent' dreams.

Only the insurance broker seemed not to have been affected either way.

As they were coming to the last bit of bread on their plates, and added more oil from Zakynthos, they seemed to have become more at peace with themselves.

In fact, the goose-lady was starting to smile, with pictures of taking up dancing lessons again, just for pleasure. The bald guy was dreaming of going back to university, in the evenings. The giggling lady thought that she could visit a library, for the first time in her life, and open the object with letters everywhere, called a book. The insurance broker, there again, continued to talk.

"Frightening!" Pauline said. "But there is always a little hope that people will get better!"

"You see how easy it's to manipulate people, little Pauline, with just a gentle push, providing they are already inclined that way."

"But there are exceptions." Pauline saw the insurance broker mutter between his teeth as he turned his cloud-looking face towards them.

Chapter Twenty-one

On the way back from the restaurant that afternoon, Pauline's father had remained elusive about the remark made by the cloud-looking insurance broker. She would have liked to know whether it was that easy to put a face on the Angries (perhaps they worked more in financial scamming schemes rather than teaching or artistic areas), a face on those who were controlling them, and the Clouds and the Shadows and the weeds. Obviously, the insurance broker in the restaurant seemed immune to the poison as well as to the antidote, which was not that reassuring, but there again, Pauline thought, for the first time she had seen a former Rainlight turned Angry, which proved that she had not imagined the lot. Or perhaps, an Angry could give birth automatically to an Angry?

Over the years she had heard her father, and his male friends, complain about many things in daily life that one day she would have to face, like paying bills far too often and far too high than she would welcome. She was in no real hurry to become a grown-up and see her name at the top of the letters with figures written on them with a deadline to pay them- electricity, telephone, tax bills and so on.

This was probably why, to mitigate this future pain, her father was adamant that she should learn maths, languages, literature and history with the utmost dedication, so that she could become independent and earn enough money to be relatively free. She knew that her five friends, seeing their mothers struggling every day, were in total agreement.

Still, the vision of the man in the restaurant, glancing at Pauline and her father defiantly, as if he had followed the whole sketch and did not seem to bother in the least, lingered in her mind.

"How did her father and the owner that the oil from 'Sapulakras' was poisonous? How come the insurance broker's attitude did not change once the oil from Zakynthos had replaced the poisonous one? Was he part of a gigantic organisation, what did the other members do, how powerful were they? Were they in all countries, stronger in some than in others? Declaring war on each other, all playing monopoly with the planet?"

She remembered that the Clouds and the Shadows were not that bright as they were blinded by hatred, so perhaps they were controlled by brains, Nasty Brains, who did not take risks but simply ordered them to do the dirty jobs.

One good thing, she said to herself, out of four adults, only one, that guy, seemed to be aware of the powers of the oil, as if he used it.

She was looking at her father on the bus. He did not look too worried, so why should she? Still, she could not resist the temptation and a few minutes before they reached the Moulin-Rouge, she asked "So is the insurance broker, the man who stared to us the real danger?"

Her father looked away for inspiration for a few seconds then replied: - "He's probably low-ranking, judging by his attitude, his vanity in letting us know that he had felt our presence, but yes, he is one of them."

Pauline was trying to organise in her mind everything she had learnt in that time, in just a few weeks.

"Stick to the basics, put a couple of words on what you know and the rest will follow nicely and gently!" he said, just as the bus stopped outside the Moulin-Rouge.

She held her father's hand proudly in the streets, knowing that one day, she would walk on her own, still by his side, but as she had seen herself in the Spheres off the beach of Alykes, as a grown-up woman, ready to take over the fight.

***

"How many pallets of Refugees can you take?" she asked Mat the same evening on Facetime. He was to stop in Paris with Jas in a couple of weeks and then hopefully two days later, the Refugees would find a place of safety on Turtle Island, in Agios Sostis, the Holy Right place.

"We need to cover them with the usual stuff from France and Italy, but we can take six or eight pallets, Jas told me."

"We shall spray Zakynthos oil over them as a protection!" she said.

"Like garlic to frighten off vampires!" Mat exclaimed, laughing.

They exchanged ideas as to the place where they should meet, the time and the itinerary through Paris.

"During the day, you will go more unnoticed," she said, "but if the Clouds spot you, the traffic jams will block you!"

"At night, the streets will be deserted, and we can go for it, but we shall be easier to spot." Mat replied. 'We shall have to gamble."

"It would be nice to make regular trips" Pauline resumed, "to save as many abandoned milk petits yiyis, who we call Refugees, as possible."

"I agree, but they seem to proliferate beyond control, a little like stray dogs. People get rid of their milk petits yiyis more and more often and, combined with the disastrous influence of the oils from all over the world that the Angries endeavour to poison, they can be contaminated ..., it seems that the Disease spreads like wild fire." he replied, with a worried look on his face. He realised that he had used the word disease and hoped that the little Parisian girl would not notice it.

Her puzzled gaze told him immediately that he had made a blunder.

"Sorry, Pauline, I must leave you, I am losing the Internet connection!" he said and vanished from the screen.

So, she said to herself, there is something going on, called the Disease...

***

Going by Mat's calculation, there would be room for a third batch of Refugees. This called for a Management Board Meeting!

With the children standing in a circle in her father's flat, staring at the map of Paris on the wall, Pauline told them about her father's prank in the restaurant, with the two couples dreaming of their past dreams, and of their

156

present anger, amplified by the poisonous oil and how they had calmed down when the waiter had given them oil from Zakynthos to pour on their slices of bread. She also mentioned the mysterious Disease, for which she had no explanation at all.

"We must act swiftly," she stated, "Mat and Jas are coming in a couple of weeks and they have room for a third group of Refugees!"

"Yes," Nafissatou stepped in, "the more we can save, the better!"

"How do we know there are other hiding places in Paris?" Fatima asked.

"Well," Sarah replied, "from a mathematical point of view, it's plausible: There are 3 million inhabitants in Paris, which makes a total of 30 million petits yiyis which have been abandoned over the past decades."

"But, perhaps some of them have not been abandoned and are still connected to those who choose to remain Rainlights" Aurelio commented.

"How many?" Zhi Ruo. "It's impossible to say."

"So what happened to, say, 25 million petits yiyis, if we accept this random figure, just as guess work?" Nafissatou asked.

"Let's try to put figures on a surface area," Pauline started, "if we consider a football pitch as a good size. It's 100 metres long x 50 metres wide, which makes 5000 m²."

Fatima knelt and moving her hands over the floor, said: "A square metre is roughly as big as that."

Then Nafissatou put her toes against the top line, joined by Aurelio, Sarah, Zhi Ruo,, Fatima and Pauline. The six children could stand in line along one metre, if they squeezed up a bit.

"Right, let's be optimistic and assume that sixty petits yiyis could fit in a one-metre length, without suffocating" she continued.

"Bearing in mind that some milk petits yiyis may be smaller and others much bigger" Aurelio commented.

"Now, how many can we fit on a vertical line?" Fatima asked.

She started to descend along the imaginary square metre, counting "one, two" her big petit yiyi acting as the reference standard, "eighteen, nineteen, twenty. So it would take a maximum 60 x 20, that's 1200 petits yiyis per square metre!"

"For argument's sake and to have a little "breathing space", let's say 1000 petits yiyis per square metre," Zhi Ruo ventured.

"This would make, on the size of a football pitch 5000 x 1000, 5 million petits yiyis, out of a potential 30 million, assuming that every inhabitant of Paris has lost his milk petits yiyis! Fatima exclaimed.

"And we don't know how many have survived, or how long they can survive after being replaced by wisdom petits yiyis!" Zhi Ruo added.

"We must assume that many of them could not find a hiding place, perhaps run over by cars, crushed by pedestrians, died of starvation, fell in the River Seine and so on." Pauline ventured to say.

"You are probably right," Sarah barged in, "the laws of maths are cruel, it would take dozens of thousands of Rescuers like us, hundreds of trucks like Mat's and so many places of safety by olive trees around the sea in the South of Europe, and this is just for Europe, so think of America, Africa, the Far-East and so on."

"Yes, the scale of pain is enormous…"Fatima said sadly.

"And what if those left alone the longest were transformed, absorbed, glued together, as if frozen in time?" Nafissatou ventured.

Pauline thought of the slow world mentioned by her mother. Another avenue to explore.

"We are still left with hundreds of thousands of potential Refugees, and we are only guessing!" Fatima exclaimed.

"It's like trying to empty a lake with a straw" Aurelio said, trying to cheer them up.

"I read in one of my father's books that if you save one starfish stranded on a beach out of thousands of them, it does not change anything for all of them, but it changes everything for the one you save- from a certain death to hope of life" Pauline exclaimed.

"We must find a way of saving more starfish petits yiyis then!" Aurelio commented. "We are surely not the only ones on the planet, perhaps we should join forces with other Rescuers on the planet."

Now that they had an idea of the surface area to look for, as a calculation basis, the children were staring at the map of Paris again.

"Could they have fled away to the countryside, century after century?" Sarah ventured.

"What did you say?" Pauline asked.

"Me, well, nothing, actually, century after century" Sarah replied.

"It's in front of us" Pauline said. "Paris was created in the 3rd century BC, by the Gauls, around the Ile de Cité, not far from Notre-Dame and not far from the Jardin des Plantes either."

"The Gauls were the first inhabitant of Paris, then?" Nafissatou asked.

"Nobody knows exactly where they came from, some say from Central Europe, others from Northern Europe, like Ireland and Scotland; but one thing is certain, they were here 2500 years ago." Pauline was proud to show that the hours spent in studying history spurred on by her father had not been in vain.

"And there were Druids, as we have Buddhist monks!" Zhi Ruo added.

The children were building images of Druids meditating with their counterparts from the Far-East, a beautiful image, and, why not?

Looking at the names of streets and the arrangement of boulevards and avenues on the map, it was difficult to imagine Druids walking around leaving clues behind to be found by the future generations.

"I have an idea," Nafissatou ventured. "Perhaps they did not leave signs but a place"

Pauline's face lit up: "Of course, it's staring us in the face. They were close to nature, respectful of the trees and probably felt like us about the Rainlights and the Clouds. They were also builders and left stone works, like menhirs and dolmens in many areas of France, as messages between this world and others." She rushed to an old book, with pages yellowed by the passing of time that had been on one of the shelves. It was a heavy book, size A3 at least, and she opened it on the table.

The children gathered around the table, feeling that the goal was within reach.

Pauline was getting really excited, as if prompted by invisible powers.

"Can you think of a place in Paris where hundreds of thousands of petits yiyis could stay, move from one shelter to another, undisturbed, with a few keeping watch in case of danger?" Pauline asked, looking at an old map, dating back three centuries ago and then showing the same area nowadays on another page. "A place closed to the public, or at least where there is hardly any traffic, sufficiently large to hide quickly, and with several escape routes that could be pointed by the guardians at the third floor of the Tour Eiffel, those who showed us the way to the Saint Hippolyte Church?'"

"This is brilliant!" Sarah explained. They are not hiding in, or on Paris, but beneath it"

"In the Catacombs" Fatima exclaimed, "and there is an entrance by the Tour Eiffel!"

Chapter Twenty-Two

"Papa!" Pauline started, "When were the Catacombs built in Paris?"

Once again her father felt he had to satisfy the little girls' thirst for knowledge. He smiled, as if he knew what was hiding in the corner of her mind, about the Refugees.

'Well, officially, it was the monks, about 900 years ago and it's agreed that there are 300 kilometres of galleries beneath Paris, which causes a lot of hassle to the council when they want to build underground car parks, shopping malls and so on. It's like "gruyere", you know the Swiss cheese full of holes. In a way, Paris is a very fragile city and some parts could collapse if they are not properly strengthened on a regular basis."

Pauline put her finger to her mouth, reflecting: "A little like our brains, if we don't practice a language or don't review theorems often, we forget and we lose the knowledge?"

"Exactly!" her father replied, with a joyful expression on his face. "But to come back to your question, some assume that excavations under the City started more or less at the same time as it was created by the Celts, probably 500 years BC, and legend has it that their High Priests, who were also medicine men, used secret underground places for worship and transmitting Holy Knowledge. Then, invasion after invasion, and those who did not want to surrender continued to meet, away from the invaders. So they built more and more galleries, deeper and deeper, with more and more entrances that only the Initiates knew about, and only they were allowed to communicate to the new members of the Resistance throughout the centuries."

Pauline was trying to absorb the information as her father went quietly along until she felt that it had all sunk in. She hesitated a bit and took the plunge.

"So, why is it essential to save the abandoned milk petits yiyis, the Refugees?"

"They have been the witness of past fights, they contain the thoughts, the dreams, the aspirations, and the pains of the past Rainlights. Think of them as a gigantic network from which you can download knowledge, to help you understand the present and to help you build the future."

"A little like Google or Wikipedia?"

"In a way, except we hope that only reliable information and testimonies are kept there and only communicated to those with a pure mind…"

The little girl frowned and wondered who is We? But thought it would be pointless to ask at that stage.

"I have two more questions …" she said. Her father felt compelled to comment, smiling: - "That's all, you're sure?"

"For the moment" she replied. "Why do the Angries want to destroy them? following her father's advice that a lawyer in court only asked questions when he had an idea of the answer, she thought she knew why, but wanted to make sure) "and why is it us, children, who need to do it?"

"Because if people can be deprived of the dreams, knowledge, and memories of the past generation, they are empty and obedient" he answered.

Pauline was happy, this was exactly what she thought.

"And you, young children are like magnets" Ah, this was unexpected, Pauline said to herself. How could she pick up on this one? She decided to pass and let her father carry on. "No child comes to the world thinking "one day, I shall sell cars for an obscene price, which consume a lot of chemicals, pollute the planet and fail much earlier than I promised the buyer" or "one day, I shall build machines which fail after so many hours of operation that need to be replaced systematically because I shan't bother to make spare parts for them. No children dream, "one day I shall govern a country, kill all my opponents, then if I feel like it, declare war on another and destroy it." Or, the crown jewel, so to say, no children fantasise:- "one day, I shall steal from as many as I can, make heaps of money, enslave people and earn even more when I am asleep because my slaves are working for me." These are just a few examples of what happens to Rainlights when they lose their milk petits yiyls and become Angries.

"So, do we all become Angries? The little girl asked, frightened.

"No, but it's that easy. You see, Petite Pauline, nothing, or hardly anything in life, is totally black or white. The Rainlights are very close to absolute purity and the Angries are more or less close to absolute darkness of mind, but there is always the chance of moving the cursor."

"You mean like on a screen, when you move the mouse to shift the arrow from left to right?"

"Exactly, some children stay close to Rainlights, others shift towards the Angries, others become Heads of the Angries, and others are simply Followers."

"So, children have the mission of saving the Refugees because we shan't soil them, because we have not had the time to shift, or not very much, towards the Angries. We have not moved the arrow of our minds, from the left of the screen, where we find the world of innocence, to the right of the screen, the world of adults, where innocence has almost disappeared?"

Her father joined his hands and clapped them gently, gleaming with joy.

***

So the Catacombs were a Holy Place, originally, Pauline thought, a little like Agios Sostis, then.

Time was getting close to Jas and Mat's trip, so she and her five friends had to find out how to get in, discreetly, and then time the sequence of operations with caution, so that Jas and Mat could take as many as possible.

"What will happen when they are on the road?" Nafissatou said that evening during their usual brainstorming session.

"It's a gamble," Pauline replied. "We don't know whether it's a trap or not, whether they are waiting for thousands of Refugees to be exposed so that they can crush them!"

"Which would mean that we have been used!" Aurelio exclaimed.

"We must be prepared for confrontation with the Clouds, the Shadows and perhaps the Angries, in the flesh!" Zhi Ruo answered, quietly.

"But right now, we must find the Refugees in the Catacombs."

So they all looked at the map on the wall and the old book spread open on the table.

"The galleries beneath Paris started 500 years BC, with the Druids, so look for Celtic signs," Sarah added.

"Yes, something that the next generations would be able to recognise regardless of language," Nafissatou continued.

"They were close to nature, yes?" Fatima asked. The children nodded. "So we should also look for signs referring to nature, like symbols of earth, air, water and fire."

"Something that would not be destroyed" Zhi Ruo commented. "More and more galleries have been added over 2500 years, perhaps the keepers of the secrets left hints, directing to the past entrances."

"Yes, we can assume that some galleries collapsed, or that some places that people could enter became built up and the entrances were blocked."

"Also, the language spoken in France has changed several times due to many different invaders" Pauline said, remembering one of her father's lectures. "French only became the official language in 1528, or 1529, I'm not sure."

"What if the first builders drew signs, then explained what it meant to the next generation, who put them into words, or a code, in the language of the time, and then translated them for the next generation and so on,?" Sarah said.

"Perhaps they build edifices, fountains, parks or holy places with names that have been translated many times over and refer to Earth, Air, Wind and Fire ..." Nafissatou concluded.

"Let's look up the names of the streets and various edifices, we'll split the task- there are 4000 streets and probably a couple hundred edifices, churches, parks and so on- so it's about 700 items for each of us to check!" Pauline said. "Although, and I'm only guessing, we should concentrate on streets in the oldest districts of Paris, the ones no more than halfway from the islands in the centre and the circular road."

"So as a first step we will discard any names in the "arrondissements" (groups of four districts) from number 12 to number 20, the furthest away from the centre?" Fatima wanted to be sure. "As they are in the shape of a snail shell, starting with number one in the centre and then rotating gradually away from the centre, we can assume that only those with a small number saw the beginning of the excavations centuries ago."

"It's just a suggestion, an elimination process" Pauline replied.

So they downloaded the names of streets and edifices, printed the lot and shared the sheets of paper.

Each of the children started to scrutinise the list with a pen in hand.

"There are so many names with words related to earth, air, water and fire!" Nafissatou exclaimed.

"Perhaps they can be related to smaller entrances ..." Zhi Ruo replied.

"We found that there was one entrance by the Eiffel Tower, right?" Pauline said, remembering the moment they discovered that the Catacombs might be a sanctuary for abandoned milk petit yiyis. "Suppose that the various generations chose four points, forming a geometric figure, so no need for languages or signs" she added.

"When they started, 2500 years ago, the world was not a small village like now when we can talk to each other across the various continents, day and night" Fatima continued. "The major civilisations of today did not exist."

"And those who did exist, did not communicate as we do now. The religions of today didn't exist then either" Sarah said," or at least if they did, like Judaism or Buddhism, they were not present in Paris."

"But" Aurelio continued, "we have been guided to places like Agios Sostis, which is a holy place, then Pauline tells us that the first builders of the Catacombs were Holy Priests. So, perhaps the first builders, the Druids, passed the baton to people who had another religion and perhaps those who were persecuted did the same."

They all looked at each other, experiencing another of those treasured light-bulb moments.

"You may be right, Aurelio!" Pauline stated. "Here we are: Fatima from the Islamic world, Sarah from Judaism, Aurelio from the Christian faith, Zhi Ruo from Buddhism, Nafissatou from Natural Spirituality and me, well, a mixture."

"Like a magnet" Fatima said, hesitantly, "at the end of the day, you started it and you chose us."

"Perhaps there are similar multi-coloured bunches of children doing the same as us in Los Angeles, Düsseldorf, Canton, Calcutta, Tokyo, Bangkok, Saint Petersburg, Abidjan, Buenos Aires and so on" Nafissatou added, visibly moved at the thought.

"Perhaps we ought to try and meet up with them someday!" Aurelio continued, very excited.

"But for now, let's assume that there are edifices, which symbolise the Four Elements, close to the centre of Ancient Paris, possibly with reference to various successive Holy Creeds" Sarah said.

"Now the Eiffel Tower with its fireworks could obviously symbolise fire, let alone that it casts a light at night to guide the newly abandoned petits yiyis to waiting halls, Pauline resumed. "So that could be one angle of the geometric figure. It has the shape of a triangle, perhaps a modern reference to the pyramids of Egypt."

"What about Notre-Dame?" Zhi Ruo asked. "It's the cathedral of Paris, close to the River Seine, on an island, the Ile de la Cité, where all the maps of France start, like the centre of a target. Indeed, when you drive in France, if a signpost says 312 kilometres to Paris, it means 312 kilometres to Notre-Dame. Don't you think it's a big benchmark?"

The children looked at each other, trying to think which element it could symbolise.

"It may symbolise Earth, and it's on the most ancient place in Paris, precisely where the Druids started to build the galleries." Nafissatou said.

"Two more to find then" Fatima resumed

"What about the Fontaine Saint-Michel?" Aurelio said, pointing to a famous meeting place for students in the Latin Quarter, a very ancient part of Paris where the equivalent of Harvard and Oxford can be found."

"Hummm, it seems a bit small" Pauline commented. "We have a straight line from the Tour Eiffel to Notre-Dame and we have Fire and Earth. If we could find a parallel straight line, of equal length, we obtain a rectangle and we simply need to draw the diagonal and find the major entrance!"

"But look, it says on the map that the main entrance of the Catacombs is in the South of Paris, Place Denfer-Rocherault, far from the centre." Aurelio said.

"Exactly, the ideal decoy for the Angries. Perhaps some of them entered there and could never come out, remember that we are talking of at least 300 kilometres, so who knows, perhaps many more secret galleries."

"Let's sleep on it and get together again tomorrow." Pauline suggested.

Chapter Twenty-Three

« Remember that the original builders and their successors were master architects and that no part of the structure was constructed in vain, we must find a purpose that would serve as a beacon for generations and generations!" Pauline stated that evening, when the children decided to let their petits yiyis fly to the secret entrance- the main entrance to the Catacombs- hopefully hidden from public view, and especially from the Clouds, the Shadows, the Angries and the Followers.

"We have the Tour Eiffel for the element of Fire, and Notre-Dame cathedral for the element of Earth," Sarah continued. "If we draw a line linking both monuments, we must look for a similar pattern on the other side of the River Seine, two monuments, one alluding to the element of Air, but not too obvious, and the last one, alluding to the element of Water, and not too obvious either…"

"Air, air" Zhi Ruo was muttering to herself, "like the energy we breathe in, bottle up and let loose in one powerful go. So if we look on the map for a succession of large avenues, starting from a strong point of energy, like a belly, that absorbs a lot of energy,"

"And a lot of knowledge of the past" Fatima added.

"Look!" Nafissatou exclaimed. "There, it's obvious, the Louvres Museum!"

The five other children were all ears.

"The building houses treasures from the past, from ancient civilisations. It's closed on three sides and opens towards the Obelisk of the Place de la Concorde, a piece of Egyptian architecture brought from Egypt by Emperor Napoleon, the flow of air continues up the Champs-Elysées, through the Arc of Triumph and then through the economic heart of the city, "La Défense", with all its sky-scrapers, and then into the infinite" Nafissatou continued.

"That makes three!" Fatima cried out. "Now, we can draw a line from the Musée du Louvres, parallel to that linking the Tour Eiffel to Notre-Dame and see where it leads us"

"Ouah, so obvious" Aurelio stated.

The children widened their eyes as the Place de la Bastille appeared at the end of the imaginary line, with the tall statue with the Genie at its top, a column made with the stones of the prison which was attacked during the French revolution in 1789, the place where so many processions started, the best symbol of resistance that one can think of.

"Not quite," Pauline said. "What has it got to do with water?"

The joy of the children was short-lived.

"Unless," Pauline added, placing her finger on the map on the wall, "look, there is a canal, tapping off the River Seine and then going under the Place de la Bastille, to join up with other underground canals beneath the streets of Paris"

"Canal equals water and the underground canals are more difficult to monitor than the streets, and are readily accessible from the Catacombs" Sarah was relieved to say.

"So now," Fatima observed, "we have four monuments, old ones, with a historical meaning, pointing to the elements and we hope that each of them has an entrance very close by."

"So, if we are right, the main entrance is somewhere in the centre of the rectangle between the Tour Eiffel, the Musée du Louvres, the Place de la Bastille and Notre-Dame Cathedral" Pauline ventured, "although it's more like an elongated rectangle, so that it's not that obvious or easy for the Angries to find

"It's probably near a monument as well, or in a district with a lot of history, a lot of symbols," Nafissatou ventured.

"That's odd," Fatima said, "There is a place with TWO monuments, facing each other. There!"

"Indeed, you have the Chatelet Theater and just opposite the Théâtre de la Ville, an old monument facing a more recent one, but both dedicated to arts and music" Sarah said.

"And from the Théâtre de la Ville, you can see the Tour Eiffel" Pauline remembered sitting outside the café next to the Théâtre once with her father and her mother on a Sunday lunch time, as they both enjoyed champagne.

"And it's the area where the Knight Templars had their headquarters!" Aurelio was proud to state. "There are streets named Rue du Temple or Rue des Blancs-Manteaux the name of the white mantles they wore."

"And their last official Grand-Master was burned alive on the Ile aux Juifs (the island of the Jews)," Sarah continued.

"Indeed," Aurelio resumed, "they were also known as the poor horse-riders and were hunted by the rulers of the time because many of them had teamed up with the Jews and with the Muslims!"

"Well, as places full of history goes, I would say that we may have hit the jack pot!" Pauline said.

The children removed their slippers and shoes, ready for a reconnaissance voyage.

***

"The main entrance probably doesn't look like a big porch way between two big pillars," Pauline said, as the six Vs made by their petits yiyis hovered above the Chatelet Theater. "On the other hand" she resumed.

"I see where you're coming from," Zhi Ruo said. "The theatre is extremely popular, it's always booked up. So, who would notice hundreds, even thousands of petits yiyis in a loud crowd, with hundreds of people moving slowly between the cloakrooms and the bar, up the stairs, down the aisles?"

"Absolutely, and" Nafissatou continued. "We were looking for one main entrance, but what about a second one, just opposite, like a mirror?"

"Yes, in case of danger, there is a plan B, just across the road and it works both ways!" Zhi Ruo exclaimed.

The six children flew to the four other places, trying to locate potential entry points, in streets nearby, discarding some because of their names. Finally calling their reconnaissance squads back to base, to Pauline's flat.

"We are missing something" she said, once all five other children had reconnected with their respective petits yiyis.

"There may be several entrances around the four monuments, as we think there at least two by, or in, the two theatres near the centre of the rectangle formed by the four of them," Sarah ventured.

"So, let's assume that we can find these and enter the Catacombs discreetly," Fatima continued, "how can we make sure that we are not going to lose our way and that our petits yiyis get stuck and never come back?"

"And if we find abandoned milk petits yiyis, how can they be sure that they can trust us, especially if some have been there for a long time?" Nafissatou asked.

"I can't answer your first question," Pauline replied, "but the second, perhaps. We have introduced ourselves to the Refugees at Saint Hippolyte Church, there are newcomers, but perhaps they know the cicada language much better than we do and they can act as interpreters.

"And vouch for our good intentions!" Fatima continued.

"Still, once we are in the Catacombs, how do we manage?" Aurelio wondered.

Zhi Ruo and Pauline looked at each other, started to smile: "We think we have an idea"

***

Pauline was too excited to fall asleep after the five other children had gone. The plan was beginning to take shape, but there were still many loose ends that had to be tightened, otherwise the whole project would fall through, and who knows how disastrous the consequences could be.

She suddenly felt a gush of air, and a little green smoke rose from the floor, turning into the familiar whirl pool. She leapt from the bed and touched the whirl pool even before her mother materialised inside.

"Mutti!" she exclaimed a few seconds later, and without waiting for her mother to invite her in, she jumped into the green curtain of smoke.

She landed on the hills where she had already been and recognised this world, that she would call the Faster World, since her mother had named her daughter's the Slow world.

Would she ask her to explain what she had meant? Probably not. She had tried to get many answers from her father but it seemed so far that her parents, as well as her cousins in Zakynthos, simply provided handrails for her to cling to, rather than an escalator.

She started to tell her Mother what she and her friends had found out so far, although she knew that her mother had followed her progress all along. She was proud that she and her friends were doing their best to accomplish a mission they had not chosen, but which they had discovered with the greatest joy, and endeavoured to carry out with the greatest dedication.

Pauline would have liked to know more about the world where her mother was now, whether her mother too had missions to fulfil and if so, which ones? Speaking German was also a source of pleasure. She wondered what was expected from her next, in case the transport of thousands of long abandoned petits yiyis turned out to be a success.

They were both walking gently among the daisies. Pauline saw a lake in the far left.

"Do you want to take a closer look?" Her mother asked.

"Yes, please!" Pauline replied instinctively, as if pulled by a mysterious force.

Her mother took her hand and slowed down a bit, since Pauline had to make two long strides when her mother would simply put one foot in front of the other.

They arrived at the lake. Actually, it looked more like the crater of an old volcano, no longer active - or perhaps not.

Indeed, bubbles started to rise from the bottom and reached the surface, just like the vision she and her friends had had off the shore of Alykes.

She saw the ten Spheres emerge. Ten, she thought, just like the number of my petits yiyis? That's funny.

Four formed a column in the middle, with the lowest touching the surface of the water, three on each side, with the lowest above the level of the second sphere in the centre and the uppermost below the level of the top one in the centre.

"What are these, Mutti?" She deserved an answer, she assumed.

Her mother looked at her, wondering how far she could go into details.

"They are there to guide you, questions for you to ask and answers for you to find, doors to knock on, for you to open and think…"

Well, it's not very clear but better than nothing, she said to herself.

"For example, you see the Sphere in the centre, the third one in the middle column?"

"Yes."

"When you look at her, you should ask questions about the way you feel, like too much of this, too little of this."

Pauline was still frowning.

"Like, how am I doing at school, do I neglect a subject, am I sad, am I happy? Are my friends happy, do I help them enough, do I help them too much?"

"Too much?" Pauline answered. "You never help your friends too much!"

"No, you're wrong, mein Schatz, you can hurt people if you don't let them find solutions to their problems by themselves, because if they don't learn by themselves, they will fall the day you are not around to help."

Pauline was looking at the Sphere.

"It's a little like a school report, where the teacher give you marks for all the different subjects."

Ah, that was easier to follow.

"You can give them names."

"Names?" Pauline asked, really surprised.

"Yes, for example the one in the middle, that I am trying to tell you about, is called Harmony, Peace,

Satisfaction, Holidays, choose which you like, but remember it's like a place where you go to find peace, away from the hustle and bustle of daily life. Where you can take stock of your actions, good and bad, and what you can do better, what you should do better"

Pauline started to smile.

"Your life is like the pieces of a puzzle. The Spheres mirror the pieces of the puzzle. They can help you understand yourself better and better."

The Spheres fell gently into the lake.

"You can keep them in your mind. They are yours too." Her mother said, 'I shall tell you more next time. Little by little"

They walked back towards the green whirl pool, on the stretch of green grass, with the castle on the hill, at the end of a long and winding green path.

"One day, you will travel the Green Path too"

Chapter Twenty-Four

Pauline had been thinking all day about the course of action for that evening: there were hundreds of kilometres and no one knew, apart from secret societies, how many levels there were, how many exits there were, how well ventilated the galleries were, which meant that some places may have not been visited for centuries and that some intruders may have been forgotten for as long. She had also read that during the Revolution of 1789 and after, thousands of corpses had been stored there, not a pretty sight, but better be prepared for the worst possible sight than fainting and losing one's bearings.

"This is going to be our first big exploratory trip," she said as the children removed their slippers and socks. "This is how I suggest we proceed" and she explained how she saw the excursion.

So, the six squads of petits yiyis left through the skylight into the cold January night over the roofs of Paris.

They soon hovered over the Chatelet Theater, which they had estimated as the central (also secret, hopefully) entrance to the catacombs. The doors were wide open and, according to Pauline's calculations, the show was going to last another hour.

She controlled her petits yiyis, as usual with the two bigger ones at the front, followed in succession to form a V and the baby ones sucked in by the inertia of the four ahead.

There was a staircase at the far right, leading to the storage rooms of the theatre. Pauline sent her reconnaissance squad down, through the costumes, the fake weapons, the mock-up furniture, hoping to find a sign left by previous generations, ideally, a keystone leading to a vault of considerable magnitude.

She instructed her petits yiyis to start to cicada. Her idea that she had explained to the five others, was that as they emitted waves of air, they might be used like a sonar radar system. It was a long shot, but they would soon know.

Pauline's V-squad was wandering through the corridors of the storage area, waiting for the rest of the team to be posted as planned.

Before Pauline continued her exploration from the storage area down to the unknown, Zhi Ruo moved her V-squad as vertically as possible with respect to Paullne's squad, above the roof of the theatre and waited. Her petits yiyis soon felt vibrations from below, like a kind of walkie-talkie. So far, the idea was proving correct. Pauline and Zhi Ruo's petit yiyis could communicate in spite of the vertical distance and the building materials that the waves they emitted had to traverse.

The next stage consisted of posting the other four squads of petits yiyis in the four cardinal points: Nafissatou in the North, Fatima in the East, Aurelio in the South and Sarah in the South, creating a kind of triangulation system known to the sailors and pilots.

Zhi Ruo was in the centre and would act as an invisible cord for Pauline to cling to, reacting to the information sent by the four other children.

181

Pauline, thus reassured, decided to hug the different walls, emitting vibrations, hoping that any of the four children would capture them from their respective sides.

Suddenly, Pauline received a message from Zhi Ruo. There was a hollow sound from the left. Pauline followed her instructions and flew back in front of a painting, with two pillars and a kind of Egyptian eye with flames blazing from a triangle. She had seen it in an opera before. Yes, she remembered, the Magic Flute.

She moved closer, and felt a little air coming through the eye in the painting. She hesitated a little.

"You can go," Zhi Ruo said, "there is a ventilation pipe, like a riser."

Pauline took the plunge, this time down into a stone flue and increasing darkness. Each of the squads positioned in the four cardinal points were cicada-ing vibrations down through the theatre and the various layers of materials, so as to keep contact with Pauline.

The hole was of such dimension that no human could follow the abandoned milk petits yiyis, it must have been constructed by Rescuers and the secret well preserved over the centuries.

She landed in what seemed to be a gallery.

They had no drawings of course, so they had to rely on the waves sent and returned to determine the depth of the passages, the thickness of any walls. It was a labyrinth, with layers accumulated over the centuries, with so many purposes that some walls must have been destroyed, collapsed, added, and rebuilt with materials of various strength. If a wave, sent like a beam, bumped against an obstacle it was returned quickly and the owner of the squad above would notify Zhi Ruo at once that Pauline, below her, shouldn't proceed but wait for a positive sign from any child, whose beam took longer to be reverberated.

Now started the really difficult bit, moving around but making sure she was able to find her way back to the rising pipe through the painting, leading to the storage area.

At first, it proved a slow process, but gradually, Pauline could follow Zhi Ruo's instructions, which were constantly updated.

They knew that the first twenty metres above Pauline's squad were taken up by parking spaces, sewage ducts, metro stations and tunnels, so they had to find a much deeper place, perhaps another chute or flue, like a well, in the midst of the maze.

They started to guide Pauline towards the North, widening their beams so as to acquire a 3D-view, or, to be accurate a 3D-feel.

Patience and perseverance have always been the keys to success, so they combed every possible direction, in front, to the right, to the back, and towards the left, in case they met a dead end.

Pauline reached the level below modern times and could smell the heaps of bones left more than two centuries ago.

She wished that all their petits yiyis had a built-in flash drive to store the directions for next time, but for now, she needed to know whether their hunch was right: were there any long abandoned Refugees hiding around there? Would she need to go deeper? How long could they survive?

She paused for a moment and gave the signal to those in the air. They started to cicada in tune. They had long debated about a melody that would stay through the passing of time, something that the Resistants of all time could recognise immediately.

Now came the time of truth: they started to "cicada" the first bars of the national anthem, the Marseillaise: tee-yee-tee-tee tee-tee-tee-teeeeee-tee-tee tee-yee-tee-teeeee tee-tee-tee.

Nothing, no response from the dark.

"Again!" Pauline said. "Again, louder!"

This time, a little echo came from the left, a few metres below, or was it a product of her imagination.

"Hang on, I think I heard something" she said. "Guide me to the left, down the next corridor, there must a little passage"

The four squads sent information to Zhi Ruo who moved above the ground and Pauline simply need to tag along as before.

She stopped and once again, the six V-squads started to cicada "tee-yee-tee-tee tee-tee-tee-teeeeee-tee-tee tee-yee-tee-teeeee tee-tee-tee".

It was not a dream, a faint echo reached Pauline. Then a little louder, as if abandoned petits yiyis were waking up. For an instant, Pauline feared that it might be a trick by the Shadows, but then, were they that bright?

She would soon know for sure. She asked Zhi Ruo to guide her a little more to the left.

They all cicada-ed the beginning of the Marseillaise again, and now, hundreds of petits yiyis were replying, faintly but with all their hearts.

Just as Pauline and her friends had experienced with the first group of Refugees in a basement close to the Moulin-Rouge, she hoped that they would be able to communicate.

The children started to breathe slowly and concentrate, ready to receive any input to form images in their minds.

Slowly, they could see masses of people, killing each other, hate-filled shouts, and women crying, trying to escape, falling and staying down. The clothes worn by the tormenters and the tormented changed with the centuries, but not the cruelty.

They saw over two hundred years of French history in a few minutes, with a few smiling faces, helping others, heroes hiding the weak. Pauline even thought for a second that she recognised a few familiar faces, but they faded into others too quickly.

Anyway, the point was that they had found a huge colony of Refugees, with their stock of memories of the past, which needed to be preserved at all costs.

There was still one question to solve: how to let them know that their trial would soon be over (there was no guarantee, but one step at a time)?

They needed to come back with some of the new Refugees from Saint Hippolyte Church, assuming that they would look more trustworthy- recently abandoned admittedly, but abandoned all the same- than Pauline and her friends, which were still connected to and cherished by their respective owners.

Pauline thought for a moment that she might leave both her baby yiyis as a token of her sincerity, but it might prove a little impractical to walk tomorrow!

"Let's bring a few with us and take them to the church on Avenue de Choisy!" she exclaimed.

Zhi Ruo guided her closer to where the ancient Refugees had sung, back with the greatest energy. She moved slowly above them, almost landed, then rose again, a few centimetres, cicada-ing gently. She could feel a few vibrations below. Perhaps they were debating what to do, wondering whether it was a trap or a genuine good gesture?

Pauline and her friends were endeavouring to ooze as much kindness through their cicada-ing as they could.

After endless seconds, Pauline could feel a little wave of air below her. She signalled to Zhi Ruo to be brought back up and out of the catacombs, through the Chatelet Theater, with a few ancient petits yiyis hesitantly following her.

The flight back up the long rising pipe, then into the storage area and out of the theatre was easier. Pauline saw that only three squads of ten petits yiyis had followed her. It was probably the first time in many years that they were out of their hiding place. They revolved around themselves, amazed at the view, the lights of the city especially appeared to blind them. Their flight was gawky at first, but the smell of freedom and the promise of a new lease of life invigorated them. Why only three squads? Pauline thought. But there again, it was very wise, because in case of danger, one squad could fight, even sacrifice itself, a second act as a decoy and the third one could fly back and warn the colony.

Actually, how old were they? Surely not two hundred years old? Now wasn't the ideal time for chit-chat so Pauline would have to wait once more for answers to her questions.

The three squads of old Refugees were met with friendly hugs from the children's petits yiyis, who placed themselves as a protection around them during the flight.

The children's squads did not move too fast, to mark their respect and assuming that physical exercise mustn't have been too frequent in the darkness of their sanctuary.

They arrived at the corner of Rue de Tolbiac and Avenue de Choisy a few minutes later.

"Wait," Pauline said. "Let me go ahead, with Zhi Ruo a few dozen metres behind, in case of danger, you bring them back and we meet again at my flat."

As she was flying closer, Pauline had the impression of seeing Shadows along the avenue, going from one tree to another, as if to check whether any Refugees were hiding in the soil, under the grid surrounding the trunks.

She flew back and said "Let's take a longer route, via Rue Caillaux, the Shadows are here!"

They landed behind the Church and started to cicada their presence. A few petits yiyis came out and greeted those from the past. They motioned them to come in, before the Shadows could see them.

"One more thing and we can go home!" Pauline said.

They flew back towards the River Seine and the Jardin des Plantes, where they had hidden the first group of

Refugees, those that Pauline had discovered, when she had followed her petits yiyis for the very first time.

"You look tired!" Zhi Ruo said to Pauline. "Let me do it!" She went into the greenhouse, making sure that neither Shadows nor Clouds were in the area.

She landed on the soil where they had spread the pure oil as barrier against them.

"Be ready," she said to the Refugees, "you are leaving tomorrow! It will be a long journey!"

***

"More haste, less speed!" Pauline said to her friends, back at her flat. The children were exhausted, but happy. They had found a huge colony, lost in the labyrinth of Time.

"Now we need to bring them to Zakynthos" Fatima said.

"Jas and Mat will be on their way from the North of Europe tomorrow," Pauline.

"What's the plan?" Sarah asked.

"Well, it seems that at long last a few Rescuers of Higher Grade are willing to give a hand" Pauline answered. "I have told them about the four monuments in Paris, symbolising the Four Elements, and the main entrance situated in the centre of the elongated rectangle.

An invitation to FaceTime came up on her computer. It was Ruby.

Pauline told her about the huge colony hidden in the catacombs, so that ample room should be provided for. Some Refugees might be very weak, so large quantities of pure oil might be a good idea.

Ruby was listening very seriously. Pauline was dreaming that perhaps one day, once she had proven her dedication and capabilities, she too could be in charge of a large rescue operation like that.

"Listen carefully!" Ruby exclaimed. And she started to explain in detail the sequence of events for the following night, and days.

Chapter Twenty-Five

The big day, or rather the big night, had arrived.

"How many are we talking about?" Jas asked, the transporter, who regularly drove his truck from Zakynthos to the North of Europe for people to adopt stray dogs from the island and then drove back, with food and wines for the expats, as he kept a watchful eye on the dark streets.

He was on his i-pad, with Mat, Ruby's older brother, somewhere in Paris.

"From the testimony that the new Refugees from Saint Hippolyte Church have received and passed on to us by our petits yiyis, several dozens of thousands, perhaps close to 60 thousand!" Pauline replied. She realised it was not that many to have sustained the passing of Time, but it was better than none at all.

"Good, if you can place a thousand petits yiyis on a square metre without squeezing them, on pallets, each one a square metre and put the pallets on shelves, we can take them easily, actually, we have room for quite a bit more, just in case."

It was Ruby who had had the general idea.

"Shall we get started?" Jas asked.

The six children quickly removed their slippers and socks, this time not for a dress rehearsal, but for the real thing and they knew that there would not be a second chance.

They flew directly to the Jardin des Plantes, where the first Refugees from the basement near the Moulin-Rouge had been waiting for a few weeks.

Uncle Yorgi was waiting with a truck, with the doors wide open. Pallets with soil and sawdust were ready to welcome the first group of Refugees. Zhi Ruo entered the tropical greenhouse while the other children's petits yiyis hovered above the garden, watching in case the Clouds or the Shadows turned up.

The Refugees from the greenhouse followed her and took their place in the pallets. To give them some energy for the long trip ahead, Uncle Yorgi spread the pure oil from Katastari, from his own olive trees, all over them, closed the doors and drove off. The transfer had taken a few minutes.

He followed the left bank of the River Seine for a few metres, then turned right, towards the Place d'Italie and down the Avenue de Choisy. The six V-squads followed him, spread apart in the night sky, on the alert. Nothing so far, too good to be true.

Uncle Yorgi stopped at the bottom of Avenue de Choisy, outside Saint Hippolyte Church. The V-squads landed behind the church and motioned the Refugees to come out and into the back of the truck.

Suddenly, Fatima exclaimed: "They're here!" Indeed, one Shadow appeared from behind a skyscraper across the road. Then two, three, a dozen, with Clouds above them, easily recognisable by the growing stench they generated.

Uncle Yorgi made sure that all the Refuges from the Church were inside the truck and drove off.

He turned right towards Place d'Italie, then left towards the Périphérique Sud (south circular.) He was heading for Lyon, about 500 km away, so probably 4 hours at this time of night, with a truck filled with hundreds of petits yiyis, and a growing flock of Shadows and Clouds following him.

Every time he had to slow down because of the traffic lights, he could smell their stench. He was breathing through a handkerchief profusely dowsed with his oil and this prevented the reeking odour of the Clouds and Shadows from stifling him.

The children's petits yiyis had stayed behind, at the foot of the church.

Ruby had advised that it would be too dangerous to follow her father's truck and they had to make a crucial choice, a gamble.

Pauline and her friends, after a few minutes, flew back towards the centre of Paris, towards the Chatelet Theater. Zhi Ruo assumed her position at the vertical above the edifice and as in the previous night, the four other children took their posts in the four cardinal points, Nafissalou in the North, Fatima in the East, Aurelio in the South and Sarah in the South, so as to help Pauline find her bearings down below.

Pauline's petits yiyis waited for them to be ready and then dived between the gates of the theatre, then onto the far right and down the stairs leading to the storage area, and up to the painting with the two pillars and the all-seeing eye, then down the pipe and onto the group of Ancient Refugees.

It was physically impossible to have sixty thousand Ancients flying back up the narrow twenty-metre pipe, some of them probably exhausted and lacking practice

192

in the art of gliding over the roofs of Paris, not to mention the blinding light, the fumes of cars, blaring klaxons and high buildings, all of which might pose major obstacles and time was an essential ingredient.

Also the Clouds and the Shadows might realise at some stage that the children were not with Uncle Yorgi.

During the day, Pauline received a message from Ruby which had filled her with hope. It was a long shot, and it had to be checked out, so during the intermission in the afternoon she explained the second part of the night to come's excursion to her friends. Once Pauline felt that all the Refugees were ready. She cicada-ed them to follow her. This time the four children's toes surrounding Zhi Ruo's had moved ahead of her, towards the Place de la Bastille, straight ahead from the Chatelet Theater, like a vanguard team. Their mission was to send route information to Zhi Ruo for her to pass on to Pauline down below, so that the huge colony wouldn't waste time in the labyrinth and could follow a trajectory without meeting with dead ends or major obstacles.

Pauline was progressing slowly, to the right, straight on, then to the left. The journey would not be more than a couple of km, in the dark, through narrow passages for humans, but wide enough for a few dozen petits yiyis in a row, which enabled them to gather confidence, looking at each other's efforts and spurring each other on.

"You're almost there!" Zhi Ruo said. The four other children had worked well and indeed, soon, Pauline could see a light at the end of a tunnel. They arrived at a Canal, the one flowing under the Place de la Bastille and joining with the River Seine, to the right.

Mat and Jas, in the meantime, were waiting on a barge that a friend had lent him for a few days. To speed the process of the transfer, he had installed a kind of soft toboggan leading directly to the cargo bay, filled with soil and sawdust, on which he had poured generous quantities of pure oil from Zakynthos.

Pauline's petits yiyis stepped aside and flew to the back, to gently spur on the ancient Refugees, who had surely not moved so much for decades, perhaps some of them from the time of the French Revolution.

Ruby and Jas had studied the fluvial network carefully and his friend, who had lent him the barge, had given a few tips to drive the embarkation to Lyon, but, unlike Uncle Yorgi's truck, a barge could only cruise at a maximum 20 km/h, so a full day at least, was set aside for the trip.

Pauline tried to count how many thousands of petits yiyis were sliding down the toboggan into the cargo bay of the barge, but no, it was impossible. When she saw that no more were approaching, she hailed her friends and the 6 V-squads entered into the tunnel, just to make sure that none of the ancient Refugees had collapsed so close to salvation.

Indeed, a few were running out of steam. So the children started to breathe in deeply, and out only a little, so as to bottle up energy. When their stomachs were filled with air, they expelled as much air as they could, hoping that the energy would be transmitted through their petits yiyis to the weakest of the Refugees. They hobbled along, helped by the six V-squads, reached the toboggan carefully and slid down.

"Let's hope we've got all of them!" Pauline said.

The V-squads left, the agreed-on signal for Mat and Jas to start manoeuvring the barge away from the mooring station, ahead for some hundred metres, then left onto the River Seine with hundreds of thousands of ancient Refugees, two hundred years of Memories, of Hope and Resistance.

***

Back at Pauline's flat, the children felt relieved. So far, so good. Uncle Yorgi had the two small groups, the one from the Moulin Rouge that Pauline had met at the beginning of the adventure, and the second one, that the children had found, when they had followed the beam from the Tour Eiffel.

How many thousands of petits yiyis were still to be saved in Paris?

Perhaps they had started with the most ancient, those who needed help more pressingly than the younger ones.

Pauline was a bit frustrated. Indeed, for the first time since she had discovered the peculiarity of her petits yiyis, she felt that she was not in control.

Of course, she trusted Jas, Mat and Uncle Yorgi and recognised that Ruby was more advanced than her. Perhaps Ruby had to go through the same motions when she was Pauline's age, and as a reward, she had been promoted to greater responsibilities.

The six children were silent, worried, but there was nothing more they could do, except hope for the best and be ready for any further challenges.

After a moment, Pauline received a text on her phone. Jas and Mat were a few km away from Paris, moving slowly and as far as they could see, they had not been followed.

On the other hand, Uncle Yorgi had Clouds and Shadows tailing him. He did not want to be stopped, let alone have his driving licence removed and, even worse, his truck confiscated and impounded by the police, should he exceed the speed limit!

He could see, and especially smell the Clouds and the Shadows, but thanks to the handkerchief over his mouth and nose, on which he frequently poured a few drops of oil, he would not throw up. The Clouds moved in the sky and the Shadows glided along the lanes, a few metres only above the cars, which were getting scarcer and scarcer, as he was driving into the night away from Paris.

The children would have liked to stay with Pauline until the Refugees were really out of danger, out of France in fact and onto the Mediterranean Sea.

"Go to bed, I'll text you if anything crops up!" Pauline eventually said. They all hugged each other, with tears in their eyes. Only now realising that they were starting to leave the innocent time of childhood, or perhaps not.

Once in bed, she placed her phone on the little table beside her. Uncle Yorgi should be in Lyon in about three hours and it was there that the Shadows and Clouds might attack the two groups of Refugees, when they saw him stop the truck to unload his precious cargo.

She had begged Uncle Yorgi to wake her up once he was in Lyon, if only for a few minutes.

Now Uncle Yorgi was thirty km from Lyon, and half an hour later he would be by the River Rhône, one of the two rivers flowing through the city, the other being the Saône.

As he started to slow down, about to enter the city, he put on a CD, one of his favourite songs, a Corsican song of love and hope: Quelli Chi Un Anu A Nimu (Those who have nothing), very close to the Greek melancholic melodies of his island, and as the Shadows and the Clouds closed in on him, he lowered the windows and turned the volume up fully. The effect was immediate, the Clouds who were closest froze and those behind collided into them, disintegrating into shards of glass, containing hate-filled angry faces, which fell onto the Shadows behind about to catch up with the truck. Uncle Yorgi waited a good minute, reduced the volume and dashed off, through the streets, with traboules on both sides, these little lanes were used for centuries by the various movement of resistance against oppressors and enabled pedestrians to move from one building to another, one street to another, very often up and down stone steps, without being followed by vehicles.

He stopped at a dark crossroads where he saw his younger son, Joe, and his daughter, Ruby, with a few other adolescents, with bicycles and small trailers. With the help of Uncle Yorgi, they placed the two groups of Refugees, the one from the Moulin Rouge and the one from Saint Hippolyte Church, onto smaller trays on their trailers, as quickly as they could, and disappeared into the night.

Uncle Yorgi climbed back into this truck and drove around the city until the awful smell came back. He glanced into his rear mirror, yes, they were tailing him, as he left the city, he turned left, towards Savoie, in the direction of Switzerland, but his truck was now empty.

Chapter Twenty-Six

Pauline's night had been short. She had gone back to sleep after her brief conversation with Uncle Yorgi. Ruby and Joe had taken the first two, smaller groups of Refugees to a place of safety, close to the River Rhône, while Uncle Yorgi had made a few more stops in Grenoble, Chambéry, Annecy and Genève, each time waiting for the Clouds and the Shadows to catch with him and each time, entertaining them with a melancholic song from the South of Europe, which he had noticed over the years they were allergic to. It was not his first trip with Refugees. He had brought a few from the North of Europe, sometimes with Jas, when his building business was slack, during the rainy months between December and March, but it was the first time that the transfer had reached such a scale.

He had driven through Switzerland and crossed the border into Austria and was now in Salzburg waiting for his chasers to catch up with him. He left his truck in a car park and entered a Kneipe (bar) for a well-deserved coffee and breakfast with lots of sausages and cheese.

It had been suggested that he could try to lead the Clouds and the Shadows astray by driving back up towards Scandinavia, but this would have been time-consuming for Uncle Yorgi and his chasers might have suspected a red herring and retraced their route back to the various stops he had made and finally Lyon, in time to find out what he had done.

So he spent a few hours in a truck drivers' hotel then at the beginning of the afternoon, he continued South, through Serbia, Croatia, Bulgaria and finally Greece, where he could join the group in Patra, and the ferry from Ancona should arrive, hopefully with a big truck filled with Refugees. Would the Clouds and Shadows follow him that far? Would they decide to turn back and check all along his trajectory to see whether he had deposited the two newer groups?

***

During that time, Jas and Mat reached Lyon, after 24 hours on the barge. Ruby and Joe were waiting for them by the River Rhône. The barge stopped and the two groups of abandoned milk petits yiyis would join the Ancients within a few minutes.

Ruby and Joe assisted in the transfer from the trailers of their bicycles to the cargo bay of the barge. They said goodbye to their friends and climbed onto the riverboat.

Good timing was essential. Jas had contacted a couple of truck driving friends from the North of Europe, some who delivered tons of pure oil to the Greek restaurants in Scandinavia, Benelux and Germany. A big truck would be waiting for them before Aix-les-Bains in a few hours.

The barge arrived in the town of Savoie. The truck drivers were there and the friend who had lent the barge as well.

All the Refugees were transferred onto the trucks. They felt much better in a truck which was used exclusively for the transportation of the precious oil, since the walls and the air were impregnated with the invigorating fragrance. Jas's friends handed him the keys to the truck and climbed onto the barge, to take it back to Antwerpen, in Belgium, now empty of Refugees and ready to transport a normal cargo.

Ruby called Pauline when they were ready to leave, this time, by road, through the Mont Blanc tunnel, then to Italy, to the port of Ancona, probably an 8 hour journey.

The day at school was never-ending. Pauline and her friends, Nafissatou, Zhi Ruo, Sarah, Fatima and Aurelio were looking at her all the time during the lessons, in case she received alarming texts from Ruby. No, nothing since the truck had left Aix-les-Bains with over sixty thousand, perhaps sixty-five, seventy, petits yiyis, including those from the Moulin-Rouge and the newest bunch, which they had discovered in the basement of Saint Hippolyte Church, on Avenue de Choisy.

At long last, school was out, Pauline's father had gone to work, as usual. Sometimes, she wondered why her father had not offered to take her and her five friends on the road to follow the expedition, but there again, in case they were being watched, it might be another decoy.

So the team gathered again in Pauline's flat. The truck should soon arrive in Ancona and then embark on a ferry, for 24 hours, then disembark in Patra, another couple of hours on the road and then Killini, hopefully to catch the last ferry of the day to Zakynthos, at 9pm. Another day of agonising suspense.

***

One more day at school had elapsed slowly. The children hoped that the suspense would be over tonight, at 11 pm, after the ferry from Killini to Zakynthos and the little trip to Turtle Island, where Uncle Yorgi would be waiting with a few boats to bring the Refugees to their final destination.

For once, the six children didn't remove their slippers and socks, they were waiting and it was frustrating, being confined to Pauline's apartment.

Pauline was thinking of her mother intensely. A little green veil of revolving smoke was forming on the floor, as if coming from the flat beneath.

Pauline knew what was coming next and was a bit afraid, although, after what she had put her friends through, with the discovery that they could use their petits yiyis as drones with in-built cameras and Bluetooth transponders, not to mention the vision of the Spheres on the sea off the shore of Alykes, they might expect anything from Pauline, but then again, not this!

The green whirl pool grew and Pauline's mother materialised inside. The young girl could see her friends' eyes opening wider and wider, as the apparition grew in size.

"Don't be afraid," Pauline said, "it's only my mother, from a faster world ..."

It did little to calm the children down, they were petrified by what was happening.

"Bonsoir les enfants (Good evening children)!" Pauline's mother said in French, with a soft tinge of the North German accent that had never left her. The children stepped back, but their curiosity was too strong to drive them to the door and flee.

"Come on in!" she invited the children.

"Trust me, trust us and follow me!" she said to her friends and leapt into the green veils forming the whirl pool.

She was the first to land on the Green Path, soon joined by Zhi Ruo, Nafissatou, Fatima, Sarah and Aurelio. The children had left the darkness and coldness of a Parisian winter night to find themselves in what seemed like Spring-Time with flowers, especially daisies, and birds chirping joyfully.

They saw a castle on the hills on the far right and a lake, in an old crater on the left.

Pauline took her mother's hand and Zhi Ruo's, and then joined hands with the others.

The children were mesmerised.

"Where are we?" Sarah asked.

"Is it the land of your Ancestors?" Nafissatou exclaimed, with tears in her eyes. "I have heard my grandmother describe a place like this, back in Cameroun, many times. So it's true!"

Aurelio was silent, also moved, as he turned round and saw a gigantic forest, as he had seen with his cousins in Brazil.

There were no cars, no fumes, no skyscrapers, Clouds or Shadows.

"Is that a temple?" Zhi Ruo asked, pointing to the castle.

Fatima looked at the sky, and opened her hands as if ready to receive an invisible bounty.

Pauline's mother did not answer any of their questions, but simply nodded, as if to encourage them to use their brains and especially their hearts.

"Do you know what is happening in the Slow World Mutti?" Pauline asked.

"Better than that, I am going to show you."

Pauline's mother took her hand and walked on holding her daughter's hand, with the children holding hands forming a chain.

She stopped at the rim of the crater and raised her left hand at shoulder height, and started to wave her fingers up and down gently. The surface of the lake turned gradually into a computer screen. They could see the truck arriving at Patra. Uncle Yorgi was there, with his van, leading the truck, followed by a couple of coaches. So far, no sign of danger.

"Concentrate on the water, think of someone intensely, all of you, at the same time, like Ruby, Mat, Joe, Jas, and Yorgi!"

Indeed, the children could zoom in on each of them and see that they were tired. Jas looked anxious. He was building images above his head but they were a bit blurred.

"Let me help you," Pauline's mother said. It was as if she had adjusted the brightness and the sound at once.

They could see and hear above Jas's head a bunch of men, drinking and cheering loudly, talking about their jobs, smiling at each other, but above their own heads, angry faces, filled with jealousy and hatred. They were working for the same firm. The children could not follow everything they were saying because they were using a technical jargon, but from what they could understand, they were lending sums of money they did not have to people who could not give the sums of money back and lost their houses or companies, and it made them laugh and laugh. Suddenly, one of them caught sight of Jas and as if flicking to a horror channel, the images thrown out of his brain became even nastier, and the stench began to grow, from one guy to the next, like wild fire in a dry forest.

Jas was remembering this as he drove from Patra to Killini.

"What's that, Mutti!"

"The Angries have been woken up by Jas, there is always a danger when we come too close to them!"

"The situation is getting worrying" A voice said behind them.

They all turned, with questioning eyes, except for Pauline's mother.

A tall lady was standing there, clothed in a white chiffon dress. A couple of inches shorter than Pauline's mother, perhaps in her early thirties, with long hair and a face like an angel, with green eyes.

"Let me introduce you to Eleni!" Pauline's mother said. "She came, comes from Volos, in the North of Greece. Her mother has Georgian, Armenian and Turkish origins while her father was born in Zakynthos, half-Italian, half-Greek.

Why came? comes- Pauline was tempted to ask, but perhaps she had not heard properly.

There was something even more unreal than the place where they were at the moment. Her features seemed to vibrate, as if her body was not solid, more like a hologram, except that she could not see any projector.

Eleni approached the lake and said: - "Look, they have left the ferry in Killini. In less than an hour they will reach the shore of Zakynthos"

"Strange," Pauline thought, "we saw Jas on the road from Patra a few minutes ago and now, he is already on the boat, as if he has driven 80 km in ten minutes, in his truck and has jumped on the ferry!"

"You remember what I told you the first time I brought you here?" her mother said.

Indeed, Pauline remembered that her mother had mentioned a slow world, where Pauline, her father and her friends lived.

Eleni suddenly rose from the ground, hovered a few seconds above the surface of the lake, then let herself sink and rematerialised on the island of Zakynthos.

Pauline recognised the heights of Bokhali, towering over the main city, below, with its crescent-shaped harbour, Solomos Square at her feet and at the far end, the ferry port, where Ruby, Joe, Mat, Jas, Uncle Yorgi and 70,000 petits yiyis, or thereabouts, would soon land. There were also a couple of coaches on the ferry, filled with Angries, probably there for a seminar, away from their wives and eager to have a good time.

The children could feel the stench the salesmen generated, the images coming out of their heads turning gradually into stinking "scoupidhia", the Greek word for garbage or refuse left on the streets to be collected. They had reacted to the presence of the Refugees and or their Rescuers, as if they recognised that they were different and consequently, needed to be chased and eliminated.

As the ferry came in sight of the shore Eleni raised her left hand and started to whisper "yi", "aera", "nero", "pyr", Greeks words for the four elements- earth, air, water, fire. Waves were becoming agitated a few hundred metres in front of the ferry.

She repeated her invocation, her eyes closed: "yi" ... "aera" ... "nero" ... "pyr" and gradually a veil of water rose from the sea, like a huge door with its top in the shape of an arch. The shape was filled with beads, of different colours, probably three times the height of the ferry.

Eleni began to smile, the ferry was touching the "Porch". The children could see briefly the expression of relief on Jas's face.

As the ferry boat progressed through the Rainlight porch, the stench diminished and the salesmen in their coaches seemed to fall asleep.

The ferry arrived at the harbour, the truck drove out slowly and turned left towards Laganas.

Eleni looked up, catching the children's eyes. She disappeared and was back on top of the lake, by the Green Path, reunited with them.

 They could see the truck on its way towards Lithakia, and then left down the main road of Lagans, then finally right towards Agios Sostis.

A few villagers were waiting. In fact, dozens and dozens of them were coming out of the dark to form rows of honour.

Giant Turtles were slowly coming out of the water. Jas, Yorgi and his three children started to unload their precious cargo onto the backs of the Turtles. They were sufficient in number to each take one thousand Refugees.

"Would you like to welcome them home?" Eleni asked the children.

Without hesitating, the children exclaimed "Yes!"

She placed herself with Pauline, Nafissatou, Fatima on her left and Zhi Ruo, Sarah and Aurelio on her right. They all rose into the air, above the lake, then into the lake and materialised on top of Turtle Island.

They could see the petits yiyis hopping gently from the back of the Turtles to the shore and then to the grass, gaining more and more strength.

Pauline waved to Ruby who had stayed on the shore. "Was she in my shoes when she was my age?" she wondered.

"Let me take you back to the Green Path!" Eleni said.

They were back with Pauline's mother, among the daisies in the daylight of the Faster World.

"Time to say goodbye, children!" Eleni said stroking each of them on their cheeks, then vanishing in the air.

"Who is she?" Pauline, Nafissatou, Zhi Ruo, Sarah, Fatima and Aurelio asked in unison.

"She is the High Priestess of the Green Path. She protects the Island and" Pauline's mother replied, wondering whether she had not spoken ahead of herself. "Enjoy your success … you are ready for the next stage of your training…"

Printed in Great Britain
by Amazon

33228358R00120